ETCHED DEEP
& OTHER DARK IMPRESSIONS

DAVID NIALL WILSON

First Edition - 2025

Contents

Author's Foreword

I am really pleased to present this collection because it contains some of my favorite pieces, oddball tales that were published in a wide variety of markets, but that don't fit any particular theme. Some of these were actually written for themed anthologies–few of those made it into the book they were aimed at. I have always taken the high road, following themes as loosely as possible and writing stories that I feel are uniquely my own.

There are a couple of stories in this book that have seen very limited publication, and at least one, *One Off From Prime*, that is new for this volume. I have also chosen to add in some poetry–I did win an award for it, back in the day, and I still enjoy writing verse–just not as often as the muse drags me to stories, and these days, to novels.

One poem in here was written specifically for the love of my life, Patricia Lee Macomber. That would be *Dark Man*, and I also included a collaborative story I wrote with Trish years ago, *The Purloined Prose*, our tribute to Edgar Allen Poe. The poem *Mirrored Hearts* appears directly in front of the story that breaks it apart and turns it into prose, and there is a poem about Loch

Ness by none other than the infamous Angus Griswold, who also appears at another point in the story.

One of my favorite things to do with fans is the "three word poetry challenge" invented by Rain Graves, who, along with author Mark McLaughlin, I share the Bram Stoker Award for poetry with for our joint collection *The Gossamer Eye*. Several of the fourteen poems in here were written for such a challenge, where you take three words–any three words–and give them to me, and I have to use all three in a poem. Some of those *not* marked as three word challenge were still created that way, like Thanatology and Long Haired Puppies. If you'd like to see how it works, drop me a note on Facebook and I'll see what I can make of your challenge.

Some of these are very old stories. They are not written in a style I'd use today, and I've edited them lightly, but I've tried to preserve their original state. It's hard for an author to do that–to let the words go without tweaking and poking at them. I've done my best.

I hope you'll enjoy reading this book as much as I enjoyed writing it, and revisiting all these words to put it together.

David Niall Wilson
January, 2012

Through an Eyeglass, Darkly

The room adjoining Monica's therapist's office was lined with shelves and cabinets filled with bottles and tubes of paint, multi-hued chalk, boxes of colored pencils, small and large tubs of clay and putty, blocks and sand. There were charcoal pencils and crayons, markers, and flip-tablets of rough-surfaced drawing paper. Easels leaned in the corners, and sunlight streamed in a high window.

Other cabinets held row after row of toy soldiers, police, movie characters and a smattering of elves and dwarves. There were animals and trees, houses and buildings of all sorts, cars, motorcycles, buses and trains. Even a small fleet of die-cast aircraft and military assault vehicles nosed out toward the room beyond.

"Expression is the key," Monica whispered, mimicking the doctor's faintly nasal New England twang.

She sat alone at one of the small tables and tried to look interested. She'd never get out of this place if she didn't create something. She was expected to bring her emotions to the surface, direct them to her fingers, and then bring them to life. That was the ideal concept of this therapy.

The truth of it was, more often than not, Monica and her "peers" doodled on one of the drawing pads, or played with the toy soldiers and left them in some arcane pattern in the large sandpit lining one long wall just to give Dr. Brubaker something to contemplate.

For Monica, there were practical concerns as well. She rarely used the paints, because they required too much preparation and skill, and the chalk left colored dust all over her hands that invariably ended up on her clothes, marking her as surely as if they'd put a scarlet "L" on her forehead for lunatic. For the time it took her to change clothes and rid the pores of her skin of the rainbow-colored dust, she felt she wore the horrors of her past and the neon-advertisement of her therapy for all to see.

It was supposed to help her deal with *him*. Daddy. Father. Anthony Pettigrew was gone, physically, but mentally and emotionally he was as much a part of her life as he'd ever been, possibly more. The slight hope had always glimmered that, if he would die, she would be okay. If he would just go away, everything could be normal, and she'd have friends and a life. That hope, flimsy and pathetic, had been like a lifeline to her. Now she knew it as just another lie from the truthless heart of the universe.

And he haunted her.

Dr. Brubaker believed her father was a disease that could be excised, a poisoned part of her psyche that could be cut out and bandaged over. If so, the disease had spread to the doctor himself. The image of a large, mole-like protrusion growing from her temple had dragged Monica screaming from deep sleep and dreams more than once. In those dreams, Dr. Brubaker gripped the growth tightly with a set of forceps and yanked it free, ripping the roots of her mind and sanity out strand by strand as his monotonous, toneless voice droned on about "inner power" and "repression of fear."

So, the question was, what to excise today. Monica grabbed one of the large pads and a charcoal pencil. She didn't choose these because she had any particular talent for them, just because they were close and easy.

Now the problem shifted to the paper. It was empty, and white. The charcoal was dark, midnight black. Her thoughts ran deep, dark red, and would not organize themselves into any geometric pattern, or seemingly meaningful symbol she could slash across the too-bright surface of the paper.

Monica closed her eyes and placed the tip of the charcoal to the paper. She let her mind drift, and it came to rest against a memory, lines tied off in seconds and all ashore that's going ashore. She sat in her room alone. On her desk, rather than schoolbooks, she had spread out the Ouija board her aunt had given her for Christmas. Pressed into place at the back of the desk and held there by the board, a photograph of her mother watched her with what appeared to be cynical amusement.

She heard her father's deep, rasping breath as he forced his twisted, Polio-stricken form down the hall. He moved very quickly despite his handicap, and she knew now, as she had known then, that she had no time. The loud smack of his worn and battered walker on the hardwood floor of the hall was quick and syncopated perfectly with the shuffling of his feet and the grunting of his breath.

The board, or the photo, that was her choice. There wasn't time to hide both, and either might send him into a rage. Monica cried out softly, yanked her desk drawer open and tore the photo loose from where it rested. She tossed it into the drawer and slammed it into place, just as the doorknob spun violently. Her father's breathing reached a crescendo, escalating from rasping to a raucous cough that rattled the door and drove Monica back into her seat more tightly with a mewl of fear.

He lurched into the room and slammed his hand down onto her desk and the Ouija board so hard that the walls shook.

He ignored the board and glared at her. He saw her hand on the handle of the desk drawer, turned, and there it was. Poking out from behind the board as if reaching out to him, as Monica's mother might have done in life, was the bottom right corner of the photograph. It had torn.

Then he looked at the board. Sweat beaded on his grizzled face and his eyes gleamed with a wild, yellowish tint. His mouth curled into a sneer of contempt, and he picked it up, holding it out before him to scrutinize it as if it were a painting.

"Trying to talk to mommy, are you?" he asked. His voice was low, but she felt the tremor of anger behind it, and said nothing.

"Did you get through?"

He swiveled his gaze to her so quickly that she was trapped, caught looking up and unable to glance away, though her feet scrabbled ineffectually for purchase and she leaned back, scuffing the legs across the floor and knowing the ruts this caused would anger him more. Again, she was too late.

"Doesn't look like homework, Monica," he said, shaking his head sorrowfully from side to side. "Didn't you get a B in English last semester? Didn't I tell you what would happen to you if you sank so low again? Don't you have an essay due the day after tomorrow?"

The questions were short and clipped. He didn't hesitate between them to allow her to answer.

He held the Ouija board up to his ear and cocked his head. He shook it.

"You in there, Em?" he asked. "You hear me?"

He shook it a final time, glanced at it quizzically, and then turned. Like a snake, he lashed out, drawing the board up over his head and bringing it down flat on her head. The sudden impact drove her neck down into her shoulders, numbing her from the top of her scalp to her elbows.

"Nobody's home," he growled, tossing the board aside so hard that it crashed into her bookshelf and sent her collection of fantasy figurines flying and tinkling in all directions. Most of them had been painstakingly glued back together after countless assaults, and Monica granted them only a quick squeak of dismay. She couldn't see straight, and what had started as a faint tingle in her neck and shoulders had spread, stabbing into her with icy pricks of pain. Tears squeezed out at the corners of her hard-squinting eyes.

"I want to see the essay tonight," he said flatly. All pseudo amusement had departed his features, and his jaw was tight. He gripped the handle of the walker so tightly his forearm trembled. "There had better be no mistakes, this time. If there are, you will write it again, and again. There are many hours before morning."

He spun on one leg of the walker and stormed out of the room. The door slammed behind him and echoed deep in her mind, pounding and pounding on the tiny spikes of pain.

Monica opened her eyes, and the "creativity therapy" room came into sharp, sudden focus. She glanced down at the once-blank paper and blinked. Lines shivered across the surface, crude, but clear. There were letters, a sun and a moon, words. It was a Ouija board and she drew back from it in sudden, trembling horror. She had no memory of drawing it, or anything.

Crushing the charcoal pencil in a sudden adrenalin-fueled grip of her fist, she threw the pieces to the corners of the room and pushed away from the table. With a soft cry, she turned and ran, slamming through the door, the outer office, and into the waiting room behind. She was breathing too fast, her heart beating too hard, but she couldn't stop. Moments later she was out the front door and onto the street, moving toward her father's old Dodge Dart at a staggering run.

Several school children hovered near the old car, and they scattered at the sight of her, chattering wildly. Monica dragged the door open, slid inside and slammed herself in tight. She leaned forward with her head in her hands, face tucked into the steering wheel, and fought for breath. She did not turn or look back toward Dr. Brubaker's office. She didn't want to know if he'd followed her out, or if someone else had. She was not going back there. Not now.

Monica fumbled in the pocket of her jeans and came up with her car keys. She never carried a purse, and in that instant she was glad of it. If she had, it would no doubt be sitting somewhere in Dr. Brubaker's office, waiting for her to slink back in with her tail between her legs in search of it, all of them watching her. Pitying her. Disgusted with her.

She jammed the key into the ignition and turned viciously.

Her world exploded in light and sound, and she screamed.

The windshield wipers slapped wildly. Indecipherable music blared from the speakers at full volume. Monica slapped at the closest thing, the steering wheel, and the horn blared. She turned, caught sight of the laughing faces of the children, innocent moments before, now leering at her in undisguised glee. Every one of them had his eyes.

She jammed the Dart into reverse and slapped her foot on the gas. Miraculously, none of the children was standing behind her. Miraculously, no one was on the street, and she remembered to spin the wheel. She dragged the shift lever to drive and burned rubber out of the parking lot, narrowly missing a taxi pulling away from the curb, and careened around the first corner at roughly double the speed limit.

By the time she'd reached the first stoplight she'd managed to get the wipers turned off, and a moment later, after hysterical effort that nearly ended in ripping the knob from the radio, she silenced the music, as well. The ensuing silence was eerie and profound. The blare of horns from behind her snapped her back to reality, and she scooted through the light, just as the yellow faded back to red, stranding those behind her for another cycle.

Monica screwed up her courage, cleansed her mind of everything but the wheel, and the road, and drove cautiously home.

———

Monica answered the call from Dr. Brubaker's office, apologized for her outburst and scheduled her next session. Yes, it was an interesting drawing she'd left. Yes, it might be important–a breakthrough, even. Yes, they could discuss it the following week, and yes–she had taken her meds.

Now she stood on rubbery, weak-kneed legs in the hallway outside her father's "den" and stared at the heavy wooden door. Den was a very good name for this place, she reflected. She had an idea it had more in common with the lairs of wolves and predatory bears than any place human beings would frequent, but...she didn't know. She had never seen. Even after her father's death, the room had mocked her.

The police had been through it, but before she'd moved back in, Monica had asked them to close it back off. She could handle the kitchen, and the shared spaces of the house, but she hadn't been ready for this.

She wasn't sure she was ready for it now.

Monica opened the door and gave it a light shove, standing her ground. The door swung open with a creak. Nothing leaped

9

from the shadows and there was no sound. She stepped forward, reached around the corner and flipped on the light.

Monica didn't know what she'd expected, but she wasn't prepared for what she saw. There was furniture, a desk, long bookshelves, and curio cabinets, all of rich, dark wood. There were leather chairs flanking an ornate chess set, and antique slag glass panes in deep green and burgundy muted the overhead light.

In contrast there were papers and folders strewn everywhere. Drawers hung open, and every horizontal surface held something that was out of place. She couldn't have explained this sensation, but the room exuded such permanence that a missing volume in the bookshelf, or a drawer spilling its contents onto the floor, which was how the police had left the room, was a glaring affront the character of the space.

Monica had started instinctively forward to straighten the mess when two things caught her eye, and she stopped. Beside the desk, right where it belonged, she thought, though she didn't know how she knew, stood *his* walker. The black rubber handles that he had gripped so tightly, that had molded to his hand, mocked her. On the desk, beside the walker, his glasses rested. Thick black birth control frames, like the ones they forced for free on military men, the lenses half as thick as a coke bottle. His eyes had watched her through those lenses. They were part of *his* face.

She trembled, and she was certain the room breathed, that she felt that raspy rhythm wheezing in and out around her, ready to break out at any moment in a cacophony of coughing, phlegm-spewing laughter.

There was nothing. Just like in the old car, where his scent lingered like mold, or rot, the unhealthy aromas of pipe tobacco and old age mingled and imbedded deep in the upholstery. The silence was deafening. It reminded her of the silence when she'd shut off the wipers and the radio. It was the silence of a tomb.

Monica reached out and slid one of the file cabinet drawers closed. Somehow this small action broke the icy stasis she'd been mired in. She stepped to the desk, glanced down at the walker, and then, without even knowing she meant to do it, lashed out and kicked it across the room. It clattered against a bookshelf, toppled two folders full of old receipts onto the floor, and settled in a heap.

She began to methodically straighten the room. Books slid easily into the slots they had been yanked free of on the shelves. The files were in disarray, but mostly the items separated in folders remained separated, and she was able to gather them up and cram them back into the yawning drawers, slamming each one closed in turn. Before long the only thing out of place in the room was the walker, it's four feet pointing toward the center of the room. She left it right where it had fallen, smirking each time she passed it and giving it another kick. It felt good.

There was a bar in one corner, cherry wood and mirrors. It held a single decanter and four short, squat highball glasses. Monica had known her father drank, she'd smelled it on his breath and in his sour, old-man sweat, but she'd never actually seen him do it. He never drank in front of her, never had a beer with his dinner, or wine.

She pulled the stopper from the decanter; it smelled like some sort of whiskey, but her own drinking was so limited she couldn't tell if it was scotch, or bourbon. It didn't matter. What mattered, she told herself, spinning slowly to take in the office, the books, the cabinets and the desk, was that it was hers. For better or worse, richer–yes, richer than she'd thought he would be–all that her father had owned belonged to her. He would not be stomping and banging down the hallway to break her things, or slapping her, or spitting on her with his diseased drool as he screamed and screamed. He was gone.

She took one of the highball glasses down the hall to the kitchen, tossed in a couple of cubes of ice, and returned to her father's den. She poured two fingers of the rich, amber liquid from the decanter over the ice and stepped around behind the desk.

Her courage failed, just for a second, as she ran her hand over the soft leather upholstery of the chair. It was deep, cushioned, and felt far too much like skin wrapping around her fingers as she caressed it. It was slick, and when she thought of how many times, and for how many years, her father had pressed back into that leather, soaking into it like slow poison, she nearly wiped her palms on her jeans.

She set the glass on the desk, held her breath, and dropped slowly into the chair. She leaned back, her body rigid with dread. The leather was cool, supple, and the action invoked no response whatever from the room, the glasses, the walker, or her subconscious. She was fine. It was fine. It was a desk, and a chair–and he was gone.

She sipped the whiskey and gazed at the shelves and the walls, taking in each and every nuance. She had been forbidden access to this space for so long that it felt like visiting an alien planet. Her mother had never entered the room either, she was sure. She'd seen her standing outside, staring, sometimes with one hand raised as if to knock, or to grab the doorknob, but Monica was certain that Emily Pettigrew had done the smart thing–the wise thing. She'd turned and walked away, letting the questions eat away at her mind, and her heart, but protecting the shell that made her whole–for a while.

She opened the center desk drawer. There was a compartmentalized rack of pens, pencils, erasers, and paperclips. Nothing out of place. It seemed that the police had not felt the need to dislodge all of her father's office supplies in their investigation–or, if they had, they'd felt the same sensation she herself had felt when entering the room, and had just wanted it back the way it 'belonged.'

She slid the drawer closed and opened the file drawer to her right. Her heart, which had begun to drop into a calm, regular rhythm, hammered. Her breath caught in her throat, her face grew red and her throat constricted. It was all she could do not to release a long, drawn-out scream.

Leaning against the side of the drawer, the only thing *in* the drawer was the Ouija board. The very board he'd smacked over her head and thrown through her figurines. Her mind reeled and she tried, without success, to remember what had happened to it–when it had disappeared. She'd never tried to use it again–but had he taken it? When?

She shivered at the thought of her father in her room, going through her things, when she wasn't there. Running his hand over her bed, her clothes.

She shook her head. No. He wasn't getting back into her head, not that easily, not over something that happened so long ago she couldn't even remember it properly. She pulled the board out of the drawer and laid it on the desk. The wood had a slick, oily sheen to it. The letters and words YES–NO mocked her. The moon winked and she wanted to lash out with something sharp and carve that mocking winking eye off the surface of the board but she did not.

The planchette was missing. She remembered that word from the box, and the instructions. "Place your fingers lightly on the planchette, applying no pressure." The word had caught in her mind because it was odd, and because it seemed right, at the same time. Such a thing should have an odd name. Such a thing, to have the power it was supposed to have, should be hard to pronounce and mysterious.

The board was no good without it, and suddenly, irrationally, Monica wanted to make it work. She had the memory of how he'd hurt her, how he'd broken her things and screamed in her face. She even had the essay, on Byron, which she'd had to write for him three times that night–until her eyesight, already blurred from what she later learned was a minor concussion–had failed her entirely. He had hated it, but she had gotten an A+ on the essay, and he'd never brought it up again. Monica kept the paper to remind her. She never dropped to the dreaded "B" level again.

Her gaze lit on his chess set, and she smiled. She rose, walked to the board, and grabbed three of the pawns. They were tall, maybe two inches each, and slender with peaked tips. She carried them back to the desk and sat down. She held one of the pawns in her hand and slid it back and forth over the slick surface of the Ouija board, and smiled. It moved easily.

There was a tube of Superglue in the center drawer, and she pulled it out. Then, her hand trembling, Monica reached across the desk and wrapped her fingers around *his* glasses. She gripped them tightly and drew them close, turning them so that the lenses faced her. She searched their depths and found nothing. With a satisfied grunt of effort, she took one lens in each hand and snapped them down the center. A second later she'd stripped off the earpiece from the right-hand lens.

Working carefully, concentrating as Dr. Brubaker had taught her, Monica centered herself as she worked. She dabbed a single drop of the glue on the tip of each of the pawns, and pressed the rim of the lens into them, suspending it over a triangle formed of the chessmen. She held it and counted to thirty, then released. She smiled. If it hadn't been for the black color of the frames, the "planchette" might have been designed that way.

"Expression is the key," she said, speaking quietly, but firmly.

She placed the makeshift planchette in the center of the board, and sat back, staring at it. She took another long sip of the whiskey, and then set the drink aside. Before she reached out with shaking fingers she had a moment to wonder–if expression is the key–what is the lock?

She gently touched the rim of the lens and closed her eyes. Images swirled through her mind, recent memories, older ones, therapy sessions and long, sleepless nights listening for the crashing thumping rasping sound of *his* approach. With her eyes closed, alone in the darkness of her mind, the silence was oppressive. She groped for a sound, anything, and latched onto her heartbeat, which was slow and steady. Thumping. As she focused on the rhythm, it grew louder and shifted. Backbeats settled into the mix, and she drew in a hard breath.

She recognized the sound for what it really was, and her heart raced helplessly, while the thumping, pounding rhythm remained relentlessly steady. She let loose a small whimper. There was negation in her voice, but beyond and behind it, something else. Something more. By the time the planchette had begun to move in jerking, sliding slashes across the board, her whine had dropped to a low growl, and she opened her eyes.

That should have stopped it. In the hallway, she heard the deep, rasping of *his* breath and the tortured, crippled thump of *his* steps and the walker. She turned wildly to where she had kicked it to the floor. The light seemed dimmer than it had before, and the shadows were long and deep. She thought she saw the skeletal framework of the thing, but it was too dark to be certain.

Except over the board. The face of the Ouija board was suffused in the reddish glow from the slag lamp overhead.

Monica hadn't noticed before, but the center panel on the lamp was a rich, blood red, shining directly down on the desktop.

The planchette moved with life of its own. Eyes, wide, she watched as it jerked about over the desk, her finger helplessly following its progress. Monica mouthed the letters; speaking out loud each time the letters formed a word.

"Talking to Mommy again?"

She cried out and dragged at the chessmen, trying to topple them and break whatever connection had been made, but it wasn't possible. What had been light resin figurines only moments before might as well have been carved of foot-tall stone. Gritting her teeth, Monica gripped two of the pawns in her fists and dragged the thing across the board until the lens rested directly over the "No."

The walker's thump in the hall thundered. The walls shook, and everything on the shelves around her shifted and vibrated toward the edges. Books fell, and she closed her eyes again, shutting it out. She remembered her own things, the collection of figurines. They had been formed of pewter, and bronze, each holding, standing on, or in some way worked around a small ball of lead crystal. Beautiful, tiny bits of fantasy she'd clutched to her like a tiny army. She could still see the Ouija board, spinning through the air like an oblong Frisbee and crashing into that army, shattering it into tiny, brilliant slivers of glass and metal. Shattering it beyond repair, or recognition.

He was close. She heard his breath clearly from the hall. The thump of the walker threatened to split the walls and open the floors into a chasm that would swallow her whole. She tasted his contempt, but beneath it, there was something else–something more.

She pried. With her fingers on the two chessmen, gripping from the center, she strained her arms and ripped outward, and with her mind she completed the effort, digging past the surface. There were labyrinths and passageways in the darkness of her memory that were meant to slow and confuse her, but she ran down them, flying after something that retreated and skittered from shadow to shadow, always just out of sight and reach.

His eyes followed her, mocking when she glared into their depths and panicked if she turned away. The world echoed with coughing and tortured, thumping steps. Sending her thoughts back to that night in her room, she heard the board that sat so solidly beneath her fingers whiz through the air. She saw the bright crystal lines of her collection explode, and as the bits and pieces and splinters of fantasy burst into the air she reached out and plucked them, one by one, from their flight.

The coughing sputtered, and then erupted anew, accompanied by what sounded like a low, tortured moan. Monica ground her teeth and pulled. She felt as if the muscles of her forearms might pop from the strain, but the planchette moved. It wasn't much, a soft shift to the side, a light wobble, no more than that, but it moved, and she growled her satisfaction.

There was no more pretense of communicating through the letters on the board. His voice whispered in the air so close to her ear that she shied away. So close he might have bitten her. His breath, fetid and rotted by disease and death, washed over her.

"Nobody's home," he said. "Nobody but *Daddy* and I am here to stay, little girl."

"No," she whispered. Then, as the word escaped her lips, she repeated it with more force, tearing at the chessmen in her grip. Her eyes flashed open, and she screamed the negation into the air before her face.

The shards of glass, pewter and brass that had been her figurines hung in the air before her but the sight did not startle her. The knob on the door shook, the frame rattled, and the coughing revved to a roar, like the growing whine of a turbine engine.

Then the door burst inward. Wood, hinges and brass knobs flew into the room, imbedding in walls and bookshelves, crashing into the furniture and toppling the table where the remnant of *his* chess set tumbled in a long, clattering arc.

Monica grew very still. She brought the image of the shimmering cloud of dust that had been her tiny statue warriors, the shards of glass and the splinters of metal, into focus. Then she breathed on them, her single word–"No!"– followed the turbine-like escalation of her father's roaring voice until the sound of her voice screamed so piercingly that sight blurred and everything went white.

The planchette in her hand burst. The chessmen broke down the center, and the lens, still affixed to one leg and the tips of two others, spun wildly off the desk.

With staggering force, the crystal blade, formed of her memory and her will and the bits and pieces of what had been precious to her hovered in the air a foot in front of where Monica sat, trembling with frustrated energy. She screamed again and the word fueled its flight.

In the doorway, darkness hovered. There was light in the room, multi-hued and rich, but beyond the door hung a splotch of deep, unrelenting black. A hole had been torn, and through it the rasping breath and thumping walker still approached.

The dagger drove into the center, pierced it, and disappeared as quickly as it had appeared. The room lurched, as if gripped in the talons of a huge dinosaur, or tossed by an earthquake. Monica fell forward onto the desk and spilled her drink in a long trail of golden light as everything slowed and focused with excruciating clarity.

The air dissolved in a sizzling burst of sound. There was a scream deep in the center of that sound, but it was not an outward burst. The sensation was of a huge indrawn gasp of dismay, held for so long and drawn to such intensity that it collapsed in on itself and crumbled. The shadow snapped out of the air and was simply–gone.

For the third time that day, Monica sat alone in a void of absolute, impenetrable silence. She leaned on her arms and lowered her head to the desk, covering the Ouija board with a blanket of her hair. She had felt alone when she'd first entered the office, but now she knew that, while it had not been true then, it was now. He was gone.

She wanted to rise and walk to the hall to see if there was a crystal dagger imbedded in the far wall. She wanted to turn on a brighter light and look to see if the walker still lay sprawled on the floor. She wanted more of the whiskey in the corner, and sunlight.

Instead she stayed very, very still, and let it all slide away. In the ruins of her father's den, tucked deep in the soft leather folds of his chair and soaking strands of her hair in his spilled whiskey, she slept.

She dreamed of paint and easels, colored chalk and freedom, and tiny balls of lead crystal, gleaming in the sun.

The Acropolis

Myth drenched and splendid,
crumbled–food for time,
Your temples standing idle,
With cats for priests &
The uninitiated swarming
About your battlements in
Spandex vestments,
Flashing memories from
Each moment to save
& savor.
Once Gods wagered upon
Your soil,
Drew lots for
Your people
Fought and lived and loved
In your heart.
Great Neptune struck your soul,
Brought forth water

THE ACROPOLIS

Heavy with salt,
Pouring from a three-pronged wound.
Athena, from a single seed
Brought forth life,
And leaves,
martinis & shaded dreams.
To the victor go the spoils –
Spoiled walls, tarnished dreams,
And the cats hold court
In the temples of the Acropolis,
Athena's temples,
Myth drenched and splendid,
Dying…
food for time.

22:19 9/22/94

Fear of Flying

She stood in the center of the room and stared at the window. It was several moments before the others noticed. Mindy was daydreaming, and there was nothing very odd about that. All of them were between fifteen and eighteen years old, and the future loomed like a huge, out-of-control video game with no instruction book. In the face of that kind of pressure it was not difficult to understand if a girl was daydreaming.

Except that she wasn't.

Mindy stood so still for so long that Janice Wilkins walked over and waved a hand in front of the girl's eyes. Janice smiled, but the expression faded through perplexity to a frown as Mindy ignored her and continued to stare. Janice shook Mindy's shoulder and got no response. She leaned in quickly, glanced around the room to be certain no one was staring at the two of them, and whispered.

"Mindy," she said. "Earth to Mindy."

Mindy's receiver was broken, and she did not respond. She stared at the window. Janice stared at Mindy.

In a dark clearing surrounded on all sides by trees and broken by the entrances to four paths that led off into shadow, Mindy flew.

The clouds above were silver with moonlight, and below her the trees fell away to a single dark shadow as she soared. Mindy arched her back and banked into a dive. She saw the trees more clearly again, growing larger and closer. Wind whistled past her ears and dragged her hair behind her like the tail of a kite. Her heart raced.

Then she was through the upper branches and sliced cleanly between trunks and limbs, diving so close to the earth that she saw the shadowy, grey-shade flowers and shrubs that lined the clearing. She shot across, then back up again in a spiraling loop. She was afraid to stop moving–afraid because she didn't know what she was doing to keep moving–afraid because she was so high above such a dark, unfamiliar place–afraid because someone whispered in her ear, breaking through the wind, and it was the wind, after all, that held her aloft and kept her safe.

"Earth to Mindy," the voice whispered.

Mindy fainted.

They brought her ice water and a damp cloth. They told her to elevate her feet, and wrapped her in a warm blanket. They stood in a circle around her, wrung their hands nervously and watched the clock. In an hour it would be 3:30 and Mindy's mother would take her home.

They were gathered in the gymnasium. Brilliantly colored streamers burst from the center of the high ceiling and drooped in curling loops to the walls. A ball of silver mirror chips spun in the center. Afternoon sunlight shone through the windows and sent sparkles of light dancing over the walls and floor.

Mindy sat on the bleachers with her feet elevated as directed, wrapped in the blanket with a glass of ice water at her side and watched the lights. She didn't speak to anyone around her–she was too embarrassed. They said she'd been standing in the middle of the room, staring off into space, but she remembered none of it.

Whispered voices roamed through the back of her thoughts, plucking them one by one so she could concentrate on none. She thought of trees, slicing up into the sky and of birds. The breeze from an open door caught the hairs at the base of her neck and lifted them gently; they settled as the door closed. More voices echoed, external this time, and Mindy turned her head.

Her mother huddled close to Coach Reshard, who had an arm protectively around her shoulder. He whispered in her ear and she nodded in time. The two matched steps as though the moment were choreographed. Someone whispered in Mindy's ear that the two were talking about her, but when she turned there was no one there. Only the reflected glimmers from the disco ball in the center of the gym ceiling dancing on the wall met her gaze, and they said nothing.

"Are you okay, dear?" Her mother asked solicitously.

Mindy noted that Coach Reshard's arm was still about her mother's shoulder, and that her mother did not object. She didn't scan the gymnasium to see if others had noticed. Of course they had; teenagers miss nothing. They understand little, they hate everything, but they miss nothing.

"I'm okay," Mindy replied. Her words were so soft she could not hear herself speak. Her mother heard, or read her lips, or didn't care, and it was all the same.

Mindy rose and Coach Reshard reluctantly stepped aside as Mindy's mother took her arm.

"Coach Reshard?" a soft, lilting voice spoke timidly.

The three of them turned. It was Sandy Preston, a tiny wisp of a girl who wore sundresses and braided her hair. Her slender ankles were wrapped in the delicate straps of Greek style sandals. Her eyes were wide.

"What is it, Sandy?" Coach Reshard's voice was stern. He leaned toward Mindy's mother, as if to offer more support.

"It's Todd," the girl replied. "Have you seen him?"

Todd was Sandy's older brother. He was Mindy's age, tall and nearly as slender as his sister. He had a hooked nose like a buzzard and thick-framed glasses that added to his bird-like qualities. His eyes glittered behind too-thick lenses, and they burned. He often watched Mindy's legs until she felt sunlight focus through the glass and burn her flesh. Sometimes she watched him burn holes in others.

"No," Coach Reshard replied. "I haven't seen him in about half an hour."

Mindy's mother led her toward the door and away. Coach Reshard leaned in their direction, as if some physical connection had stretched, and then broken. He snapped back to Sandy; Mindy and her mother snapped toward the door. A few heads turned. Mindy was glad that Todd the buzzard would not be watching her legs as she left. She wondered if he would have watched her–or her mother. She knew which of them Coach Reshard watched.

The drive home was silent. Mindy climbed out without a word to her mother, grabbed her things, and ran to her room. Her mother ran to the kitchen, then to the television, and the phone. Mindy's dad wouldn't be home for another two days, but Coach Reshard…

Mindy threw her book and gym bags onto her bed and sat at her desk. Her window faced the back yard. She stared out past her old swing set, the chains rusted now and the plastic seat half-cracked in two. Beyond their yard and across a churchyard there was a band of trees that lined a golf course. It reminded Mindy of the forest.

The phone rang. Footsteps approached and Mindy heard her mother's voice in the hall. The words were soft, but Mindy heard.

"Oh my God, John."

Coach Reshard's name was John.

"When…are you sure? Oh my God…"

As her mother prayed, Mindy drifted. The chair fell away behind her. She dangled her arms and used them to balance on the breeze. Subtle shifts lent altitude and angle to her flight. The sunlight shimmered and died as she soared above the trees and circled.

Far below her mother's voice echoed.

"Oh my God."

Mindy dove. The trees spiraled inward, starting as a thick wall and thinning as they wound toward some unseen core. She followed the spiral and wondered who had planted it. She dove lower and skimmed the upper branches, dipped and flashed between trunks, slid sinuously over branches and back up again. She flew like dolphins swim, and always she wound inward. Tighter. Like the spring of a clock, her passing drew the trees behind her and held them taut. As she neared the center of the coil, the tension eased. The line of trees flowed behind her, swayed upright and then whipped back in a line, never touching one another as they snapped first one way, then the other, and finally came to rest.

In the center she turned up and flew toward the sky through a tunnel of green leaves and dark limbs. Just as she turned, she caught a flash of color, and it stuck with her as she rose, reached a peak, and flipped, dropping into a graceful swan dive toward the center of the clearing. None of it was powered by her thoughts. She moved. If she stopped moving, she would fall. She knew this, but did not know how she kept moving. She didn't know how not to fall.

In the center of the clearing a new sapling had sprung from the earth. Colored streamers hung from its tip. They flowed up and out and fluttered in a breeze that Mindy couldn't feel. She was moving too fast, making her own breeze. She wondered how the streamers had gotten here, so far from the gym, and where was the disco ball? She cut to her left, broke into a sweeping curve that brought her very close to the ring of trees, but not touching. She spun down at dizzying speed.

The sapling took form and thickened, sprouted dark hair. She pulled out of the dive to flash inches above the ground and turned directly toward the intruding growth.

She pulled up from the earth and launched skyward once again, turned short of the sapling and slipped up its length. She passed the center where a root wound round and round and protruded at an obscene angle, hard and dripping with sap. She gasped and in that instant passed face-to-face with Todd the Buzzard. He glared at her through too-thick lenses and ran his fat, wet tongue over his lips.

Mindy cried out and arched, hurtling toward the trees. She closed her eyes, and…

———

"I have to go out for a while, dear."

27

Mindy's mother's voice cracked and ran in myriad directions at once. It dripped concern. It was flushed with excitement. It hid secrets, but held no real concern for Mindy.

Mindy nodded.

"There are frozen dinners," her mother continued. "I shouldn't be too late. They still haven't found that boy–you know the one, Todd…"

"Preston." Mindy finished, hoping the finality would paste itself to her mother's departure and drive her away.

"The Buzzard," Mindy added. Her voice was very soft, not really meant to be heard.

"Excuse me?" her mother asked.

Mindy said nothing. She turned to the math textbook on her desk and put on a character-actor performance. She portrayed a student. Her mother clucked her tongue, spun on heels too tall for searching for lost boys and too short to scream impropriety. Moments later the door shut with a loud Click!

Alone, Mindy closed the math book, shoved it aside, and walked to her bed. She wasn't hungry, and she loathed the microwave dinners her mother kept piled in the freezer. When her father was home, the freezer held ice cream and neatly stacked packets of frozen vegetables. Some mothers were talented at bringing complex five-course meals to the table, all warm and fresh and ready to serve. Mindy's mother could plan the freezer space to allow for three tightly packed rows of microwave meals the same day her father left on business.

Mindy wondered if Coach Reshard ate microwave meals. She wondered if his freezer was the antithesis of theirs, full of vegetable packets and ice cream only when Mindy's father was out of town.

Mindy lay back on her bed. The soft feather pillow her father had given her for Christmas formed itself to the shape of her head and slid up to cover her ears. The down muffled all sound but a roaring in her ears. Mindy closed her eyes.

The feathers in the pillow were restless. They remembered the sky, wind whistling through and beneath them, ruffling them and driving them aloft. Mindy felt them buoy her up, head and shoulders first, until she floated over the bed. Then the bed and the room dropped away. The pillow tore and the feathers floated out around her. They tickled her arms and legs and teased over the back of her neck. Two large, grey and white feathers drifted across her eyes and dimmed her vision.

The room dissolved into fluffy white clouds. The feathers coated her skin, slick and smooth. They rustled in the breeze. Mindy turned and knifed through the clouds. Moments later she broke through into a gray sky and soared above the trees. Lights winked at her in the distance.

From her vantage point the forest was a great whirling Nautilus shell of greenery, winding inward to a hollow center. Mindy remembered flying that spiral, and she smiled. This time she cut to the quick. Darting straight down, she drove toward the center of the woods. She was an arrow, pillow feathers flocked the shaft of her body. The clearing rose through the branches, a tall cylindrical column with branches and leaves for walls and at its root?

She dove, oblivious to the ground below or the sky above. In the center of the clearing the sapling had grown taller. It had grown more disgusting. The root jutted from the center of the young tree's trunk nearly back to the ground. Sap dripped obscenely from its tip in a string that bridged the short distance to the tips of the blades of dark grass. Mindy ignored it and dove. She stopped so close to the Earth that grass tickled her, even through the coating of new feathers. Knees dropping first, she pressed into the earth at the foot of the sapling and trailed her gaze up its length. She was careful not to get too close to the dripping root.

When her eyes locked onto twin knotholes above a beak-shaped broken branch, she saw that they met her gaze with hunger. Black dots of intensity floated in their depths, and trailed down her body. A worm, unaware of her presence, stuck its head from a crack in the bark, just beneath the broken branch beak. It lolled to one side, then the other, as though dampening bark lips. As though hungry.

She dropped her gaze and watched the root ooze new sap.

She rose to her feet and felt her feathers ruffle. The black dot eyes followed her motion. She reached out with thumb and index finger and plucked the worm from its crevasse. The sapling shivered. Moisture leaked from the twin knotholes, but she didn't care.

Mindy raised her eyes to the sky. She gave a great cry, mournful as an owl and predatory as any falcon. She raised her foot, kicked it down, and snapped the root off at its base. She felt the slick, viscous fluid on the ball of her foot and wiped it in the grass. She kicked off and caught the breeze. She rose in a spiral, gathering speed until she burst free of the trees and banked off toward the distant twinkle of city lights.

Mindy woke to the sound of crunching gravel. She sat up when she heard the kitchen door open, and then close stealthily. She clutched her pillow tightly, and found the seams intact. One sharp shaft pricked her arm, and she gripped it, drawing it out through layers of cloth and pillowcase to rest in her palm.

She heard steps in the hall and saw shadows shift, and then her mother stood in the doorway to her room, looking in.

"You're awake," her mother said.

Mindy said nothing. She tried not to imagine the scent of leaves, and of sap. She tried not to feel the weight of wood and root cracking against the ball of her foot. Her skin tingled.

"They found that boy," her mother said. The tone of the words indicated compassion, but it felt forced.

"He was in the woods. Alone. He…"

Mindy turned away.

"He'd been through a lot." Her mother concluded. "He's alive, but his mind…"

"Snapped off at the root," Mindy whispered.

"What?" Her mother's voice was sharp and brittle. The concern in it snapped like glass and was gone.

"How is Coach Reshard?" Mindy asked.

Her mother's shadowed form grew rigid. Mindy heard long, pampered nails dig into the wooden frame of the door. Her mother's indrawn breath was a sudden hiss.

"He found the boy," her mother said at last. "He brought him back."

Mindy nodded. "You too, mother? Did you bring him back?"

A soft, impatient stamp of her foot, and Mindy's mother shifted the subject. "The boy was found with feathers. Can you imagine? Buzzard feathers. He had them in his…clothes. He…"

"Do you ever dream of flying, mother?"

Silence.

"Do you think Coach Reshard dreams of flying?"

"Honestly," her mother said softly, spinning on her heel and escaping. "I don't know why I talk to you."

Silence fell again, and Mindy lay back on her bed. She placed the single loose feather against her cheek, pressed it into her pillow, and she slept.

In the dark, with a colored spotlight trained on the spinning, mirror-shard-coated disco ball, the gymnasium was a fairyland of whirling lights and dancing couples. Long tables with cookies and punch bowls lined one wall near the door, far away from the dance floor. Mindy stood at one end of the table.

She stared up and out a high window. The window was a flat pane of darkness. Mindy didn't see it, and nobody saw Mindy. She stood alone with her cup of punch and the crowd milled around her, lost in a myriad of tiny, two and three person worlds of which she was no part.

Mindy's mother had volunteered to chaperone. She stood in the doorway, staring out over the parking lot. Then she turned and came to stand beside her daughter.

"What are you staring at?" her mother asked.

Mindy said nothing. She gave no indication she'd heard the question.

"Why don't you dance?"

Mindy's mother stepped in front of her daughter and stared deep into the girl's placid, far-away eyes. Her stomach shifted and she thought of the downside swing of a Ferris wheel. She heard something. A screech of feedback from the DJ? The cry of a bird.

"Have you seen Coach Reshard," her mother asked softly. "He was here, and then…"

Mindy stared out the window into the dark night sky.

Her mother turned away, moving back toward the door. In turning, she missed the flutter of white, glittering feathers dropping from the mirror-light splendor of the gymnasium sky.

Mindy soared.

Clamdigger

A Three Word Challenge Poem

Clamdigger / Slope / Centrifugal

He'd fallen on hard times.
The restaurant up the beach kept him
In hooch if he produced.
He worked in the evenings,
Or very early mornings,
Before the kids started in,
Roaring up and down the boardwalk,
Rushing screaming into the waves,
Surfboards in hand,
Cruel smiles on their lips.
They threw things at him.
They called him Ol' Clamdigger
And spilled his bottle when they could.
He followed the gentle slope of dunes
Down to the crashing waves.

He took his spade and plunged it deep,
Felt the wet suck of sand on the blade.
Water poured into the hole like a whirlpool,
Centrifugal force fought his efforts.
He found them on the third stroke of the spade,
Turned them up and started down the beach,
Tossing them into his basket and dreaming
Of a time before his one love was named Rose,
Wild and Irish, before his sneakers shared his
Lack of soul. Before he was nothing,
But the Ol' Clamdigger.
He didn't hear the boy slip up behind him.
When the blade crossed his throat,
He staggered. Blood dripped and stained
The clams. He turned, but
His vision blurred.
He held out the basket and tried to tell the boy
To hurry…
Or the clams might spoil.

Moving On

Jessup held the rifle by the butt, finger on the trigger. He gripped the rusty door handle and stood very still, listening. He heard nothing but leaves skittering across the dry, dusty ground. A gutter, caught in the same breeze that taught the leaves to dance, suddenly swung into the wall with a creak. Jessup flattened himself against the wall. When the gutter swung again, he caught the motion out of the corner of his eye and cursed. He stepped back to the door, lifted the handle, and opened it.

The only light came from smudged, filthy windows. Jessup swung around the door, swept the room with the gun at his hip, and scanned a little ahead of the barrel to target anything that moved. There was nothing. He swung back and lowered the gun to his side.

The old warehouse was draped in shadows. Stepping further in, he scanned the shelves. Boxes hung partially into the aisles. Packing material littered the floor. It looked as if a damned tornado had blown through, and Jessup's heart sank.

He kicked his way down the aisles, pushing the boxes out of his way, looking for anything that might have been left behind. They'd waited too long.

On one of the back shelves a single can of beans lay canted to one side. He picked it up, tossed it in the air, and caught it. He gripped the can so hard his knuckles went white, turned, and slammed it into the wall. It dropped with a dull, impotent thud. It only took a few minutes to be certain there was nothing more, and he was back out the door. The sun had started to drop toward the horizon. Not much time before it started to get dark. There were more warehouses further up the mountain, but he'd never get there and back in time. He knew it didn't matter. If this one was empty, what would the others be like, so far from the city? How far would he have to go before the fallout worked its way into his lungs and started eating his skin?

He climbed in behind the wheel of his old pickup, slapped the rifle into the rack behind his head, and started the engine. Without waiting to see if the sound attracted anyone, he backed out and floored it, leaving a plume of dust as he wound back to the main road and turned toward the highway and down toward Wiley.

The lights were on at the perimeter when Jessup returned. Lonnie and Jack, the Cooper boys, stepped out of the shadows. Jack held a 9mm at an angle, not really ready to shoot, but following protocol. Jessup frowned. He'd rather the kid shoved it through the truck's window and into his face and that they searched the truck from one end to the other. Someone had emptied that warehouse, and that meant someone was close enough to try and empty other things. One stupid move and their homes might not be theirs any longer.

"Get that gun up," he growled.

Jack glanced at him and a lop-sided sneer split his face. The boy's hair was greasy and dangled over his face in a sloppy part. He hadn't shaved, but he also hadn't really grown a beard. Patches of soft fuzz dotted his cheeks, and his lip looked like he'd brushed it with charcoal.

"Punk," Jessup muttered. Louder, he said, "Warehouse on Water Street is empty. Someone's been through it. That's only ten miles–halfway up the mountain. Keep that gun up, boy. No one comes in. No one comes close."

Jack stared back at him, as if ready to smart off, but Lonnie cut in quickly.

"Who?" the boy asked. "Who's been through it?"

Jessup heard the fear–almost panic in the boy's tone. He shook his head.

"How the hell would I know? It's empty, that's all I know. If it's empty, someone's been through it. Ten miles is too close, and we didn't even know they were there."

"What do we do?" Lonnie asked.

"Guard the road," Jessup said, "Like you've been trained. Nothing has changed except we know someone's there."

"What about the food?" Jack said. "If they got the food from that warehouse, they probably have everything from here to Thompsonville."

"Roads go a lot of different directions," Jessup said without conviction. "There's mountains on all sides. We'll try the North side next. I'll tell Dan we need extra guards here. I don't know if they were out there today, last week, or a month ago, but I know they were there, and that means they know we're here too. When all the warehouses are empty, they're going to try and come at us. Best be ready."

"You think they're sick?" Jack asked. He still wore his sneer, but now it lacked conviction. "Like that guy came in last month? Looked like his eyes were sinking into his head. And his skin…"

"No way to know that either," Jessup said. "If they are, they may hang back. Give us a chance to spot them. Might make them desperate. Same guy you're so fascinated with could barely walk. He wasn't much of a threat. There's no way to know where they came from, what they have, or how bad off they are. Just keep your eyes open."

Jack stared at him. "Easy for you to say," he muttered. "Not all of us have a pretty wife and a house full of who knows what to get back to."

Jessup glared at the boy, but bit back his comment. He'd seen the way Jack and his brother eyed Mae every time he brought her outside the confines of their home, and he knew the danger in it. He didn't like leaving town, but someone who could be trusted had to do the scouting.

He pulled away and turned down Main St. toward his home. He knew the two were watching him go, and he knew the second he was out of sight they'd be chattering like women, trying to figure out whether to head for the hills, tell everyone in town what they'd heard, or just stand still and do what they'd been told. He knew, in the end, it would be a combination of all of it. They'd stay at their post, but they'd find a way to spread the word. It was fine with Jessup. As a matter of fact, it was about time.

He pulled into his driveway and cut off the engine, but he didn't get out immediately. The low-slung brick ranch he and Mae had built so long ago felt like a cage these days. He sat, and he thought about the empty rows of shelves out on Water Street. He thought about the single can of beans, and wondered who had left it behind. He wondered how long it had taken them to leave their homes, branching out to the roads in search of food. He wondered if they still looked human, or if they were burned. He'd seen the broadcasts near the end. He'd heard the reports. Wiley was located in a valley, mountains on all sides, and they'd missed the worst of it. A few had gotten sick, a few had even died, but most of them had gotten off pretty easily.

They'd been approached by refugees. Jessup had regular nightmares about burned skin and ravaged features. He saw eyes staring at him from the shadows out of pits that had once been healthy sockets. Every time his skin itched, his heart raced, and he wondered if it had come for him at last. None of the strangers had stayed. They weren't welcomed, and most of them died. Wiley had no medical facility capable of dealing with their condition—and despite their curiosity, they'd learned little about what was happening beyond their valley from the few encounters they'd had. Dying men and women aren't prone to storytelling.

Now Jessup had to think that if a group of refugees was out there, they wouldn't stay away. He knew it wasn't just the food, either. They'd want alcohol, and guns, maybe women. A lot depended on who they were, how they were organized, and how desperate they'd become.

He locked the truck out of habit and walked slowly to his front door, the rifle held close down beside his leg. He hadn't felt safe walking in the open for weeks. The weight of the weapon in his hand helped, but it didn't take away the odd, burning sensation on the back of his neck—the phantom brush of eyes, watching from the shadows. He knocked and waited. There was a soft scrape as Mae glanced through the peep-hole, then louder sounds as she unfastened the deadbolts and locks that kept them safe. Jessup didn't carry keys. If he were killed, he didn't want anyone getting hold of them. Not even the others in town.

The door swung open and he slipped inside, pushing it closed and immediately reaching for the locks.

"How did it go?" Mae asked.

Jessup worked the locks slowly and methodically, ignoring her. He could have scripted the conversation to come, and he was too tired to play his part. When the final bolt slid into place, he leaned the rifle carefully against the wall inside the door and headed down the hall toward the kitchen.

"There's beer," Mae said.

Jessup spun and stared at her. Before he could speak, she went on nervously.

"Becky Springer brought it. They found a room over at the Bowling alley. You know, where they're clearing away the debris? There was a door to a cellar. The food was ruined, but there was enough beer for two cases per family."

"How'd it get in?" Jessup snapped.

She stared at him, shocked. "When Becky came, I let her in," she said. "I thought you'd be happy, the beer…"

Jessup felt a sudden blaze of anger. He turned away and leaned his head on the wall as he fought to clear his thoughts. As his mind ran over all the things that might have happened, the men and the women who might covet what he had, the anger turned to irrational fear. He bit that back as well.

"Are you stupid, woman?" he asked.

Mae laid her hand on his shoulder. It trembled.

She shook her head. "I'm sorry Jess," she said.

Jessup turned toward the kitchen. Mae's hand slipped off his shoulder. She stood and watched him go. He didn't turn back, and a moment later she followed, entering the kitchen just as the snap of a pop-top can announced the first of the beer.

"She came with Dan," Mae said softly.

Jessup shrugged. It was an old argument. The longer the city had been under what Dan called "martial law," the more critical security had become on a personal level. Homes had been looted, women had been taken. There wasn't much the community could do. Things had changed. The thin veneer of normalcy they maintained with their patrols and their meetings was wearing away.

The others looked to Jessup and Dan as leaders, but they had to create their own authority, using force, at times, and it was becoming sadly obvious that what served for civilization was crumbling to ruin all around them. Folks were either scared, or bad. Neither was a good for security.

"You remember Harry Coombs," Jessup asked. He was staring at the beer in his hand, turning the can around and around to read the label. He waited.

"Yes, baby," Mae finally answered.

"You used to play cards with his wife, isn't that right? Sarah? Was that her name?"

"Yes."

Jessup stood, grabbed two more beers, and tossed one to Mae. She was so surprised by the gesture she almost missed it. She opened it shyly and took a sip as he returned to his seat and started on his second.

"Some boys broke into their house last week. Harry's dead and Sarah...well, she isn't with Harry anymore. Dan and I talked to one of the boys responsible. Dan wanted to go after them."

Jessup paused and drained half the beer. He turned to Mae and held her gaze.

"We didn't go," he said. "We can't afford to. We can't afford to lose those boys on the watch, especially not now, so we have to let it go. Harry wasn't a close friend of mine, but he was a good man. Now he's dead, and I can't do a thing about it. Do you hear what I'm saying, Mae? Am I getting through?"

Mae's hand trembled and she gripped the beer more tightly. She didn't answer–Jessup knew she wasn't going to answer. What could she say?

"The locks on the door are there for a reason," he said. "I leave you keys so you can let me back in, and for no other reason. I lock the doors because I want to come home to my bed...and to you...and find things as I left them. You think if someone came and took you I'd be able to help? You've seen the way those Cooper boys watch you–you're a damned pretty woman, Mae. You think if they came and took everything we own, everything we have left, that Dan, or anyone else would give a damn? There's no sheriff to call. We're on our own, and now..." he hesitated.

Mae glanced up, and Jessup sighed.

"Now it may all be for nothing."

"What do you mean?"

"Warehouse was ransacked," he said shortly. "Someone's been there, and it wasn't anyone from here. We'd know. Someone would have let it slip."

"But who?" Mae asked.

"Don't know," Jessup said with a sigh. He drained the beer. "Don't know, and it doesn't matter. We can't stay here. We'll be out of food by winter, and if we wait any longer, there won't be anywhere to go. People are moving out there, and they'll want what we have. We don't know how bad it is out of the valley, not really."

Mae clutched her beer and dropped her gaze to the floor. He didn't know if she was imagining being taken by local boys, or thinking about the sick ones–the ones the radiation had gotten to–slinking around in the hills. When she finished her beer, Jessup got up and handed her another.

"Let's get some rest," he said, his voice softer. "We'll need to meet with Dan tomorrow, and the others."

"What will we do?" she asked.

"What else can we do?" he replied. "We'll have to leave. We'll have to go, like they had to go. We'll have to find food, and we may have to be ready to take it."

Mae watched him for a while, drinking her beer, as if she thought answers might flit across his face, but Jessup paid no attention. He was lost in thought, trying to plan for something no one could predict. How did you plan to leave without knowing where you were going, or what you'd find when you got there? He had a sudden, intense craving for baked beans.

———

They met, as usual, at the jailhouse. There was no good reason; all the equipment had long since been stripped away. The gun cabinets were open, the ammunition had been distributed. Jessup thought maybe it was the bars on the windows, or the cells in the back. They'd managed to set up four or five surveillance cameras on the main routes into town, and the monitors at the station could be run off generators. They had gas–used carefully it would outlast the food, maybe even the alcohol. The city had experimented ahead of its time. An extensive network of solar batteries handled most of the homes–at least enough for those who remained in town.

Wiley was a fortress under siege by entropy. The valley was bordered on all sides by mountains, which had blocked most of the fallout. Without road maintenance, and with more and more abandoned vehicles lining the roads in and out, Mother Nature had taken her normal course. The valley was all but sealed off from the world. Food was running out. They could get some water from a stream running down from the west, but there was no way to know if it was clean, and for the most part they'd left it alone. They couldn't do it much longer, and no one wanted to think about what happened if it was dirty.

So things crumbled. Bit by bit. Jessup, Dan, and a few others fought for stability. They tried to maintain order, forced a weak, diluted form of martial law on the town to keep it in line, but their efforts were doomed. Without laws and a government, Darwinian rule leaked into their society bit by bit, and there was no way to stop it. The city was too much like a cage to the young, and too feeble a fortress to the old.

The 'council' gathered around the conference table in the Sheriff's office. Dan sat straight and tall, his back so stiff his spine could have been a two-by-four. His hair was clipped short in the same style he'd worn in the marines, even though he had to do it himself. His eyes were flat and colorless, and he sat apart from all the others. He and Jessup had been friends for a decade, but now? Jessup would once have trusted Dan with his life but, but now there were questions. It was getting harder to trust anyone.

The rest of the group was a mixed lot. Lonnie and Jack Cooper were there, and Brian Winslow, who'd run the hardware store. The last of them was old Tish Maynard. She'd been the head nurse at the clinic–Wiley wasn't big enough for a full-blown hospital. Doc Jenkins took off early on, panicked over family back east. Tish was the doctor now; doctor, nurse, and tough as nails.

"So," Dan started them off. "We aren't alone. I didn't figure it would take long."

Jessup nodded. "Looks that way, Dan; that warehouse was cleaned out, and it's not far out of town. Whoever it was was quiet."'

"They didn't want us catchin' them," Jack suggested. His eyes glittered with that sparkle young, stupid men get when they think about fighting, and war. "They were scared."

"Or they didn't want us to know they were coming," Brian Winslow cut in. "Don't get too full of yourself, Jack. There's folks out there a whole lot worse than you think you are, and they won't be shy about proving it when you meet. Not anymore."

Jack glared at Brian, but for once he kept his peace. He glanced at Lonnie, who met his gaze for a second, then looked away. Jessup frowned. Something had been communicated that the rest of the group wasn't privy to, and it couldn't be good. He filed the information away and cleared his throat.

"I think it's time we admitted Wiley is dead, or at least dying. We have to pack up, gather what we have, and hit the road."

"Where?" Tish asked. She met his gaze levelly.

"To somewhere else," Dan cut in. "Jessup's right and you know it. There have to be others out there, cities, military bases. We get out past the hills, we should be able to pick up some kind of broadcast. We can't stay here forever. Food is scarce, and with winter coming, sitting here on what we have left until we starve is suicide. Either we'll run out and have to leave anyway, or someone bigger and badder will come in and take it."

The silence was thick enough Jessup felt stifled.

"What do we do?" Brent Winslow asked. "What do we take, and how do we get out? The roads are bad—it'll take time to clear them, but if we don't drive out, we'll have to leave too much behind."

"We drive," Jessup said without hesitation. "We've got trucks, and we've got plenty of equipment and tools, for now. We wait too long half of it won't work, but now it does. We take a bulldozer along to the top of the ridge, cut a path through to the freeway, and we move on from there."

"To where?" Tish repeated.

"West," Dan cut in. "There's an Air Force base 100 miles west. If no one's there, we may be able to pick up some supplies, and we head on south and west, toward the gulf."

"Why?" Jack asked.

The sneer was back on the boy's face, and Jessup wanted to smack it loose, but he held his peace. Dan had it under control–the two of them had talked this through, and Dan's logic was sound.

"Simple," Dan replied. "As long as we avoid the base in San Diego, there's not much down there they'd try to hit. Shouldn't be as hot in uninhabited areas as it is in the cities. Like here. We're not close to anything–first time in my life I ever saw it as a good thing."

"It's why we should stay," Tish spat. "I don't like it. We don't know if there's a damned thing past those hills. Here? We have some water…maybe. We have some food, and if we're careful, we can grow more. For all we know everything past the mountains is hot, or dead."

"You know that's not true," Jessup said. "It hasn't been that long since the broadcasts stopped, Tish. They're out there, and we need to find them–a group large enough, and stable enough, to take us in."

"I say we go," Jack said. "There's nothing here. Anything we find is better than sitting here."

Dan and Jessup turned and met the boy's gaze. He didn't drop his eyes.

"Anything," he repeated.

"So we vote?" Tish asked.

Dan nodded. "I'm for going," he said.

Jessup raised his hand. Jack and Lonnie were next, and slowly, everyone in the room raised their hand but Tish. She shook her head slowly, but Jessup knew she saw it too. She'd been living in Wiley all her life. The house she still lived in was the house she'd grown up in. For all her strength, leaving terrified her.

"When?" Jack asked.

"We pull the trucks in today," Dan said. "Get some heavy equipment fueled and checked out. No reason to push it, but it's time to get started."

"Maybe there's some women out there," Jack said, his voice low.

Tish turned on him like a snake, ready to strike, and he held up his hand in mock defense.

"I'm just saying," he continued. "Food and water ain't the only things we're short on here. At least some of us are short of it, anyway."

Jack glared at Jessup, who reddened, but remained silent. The boy was right, and he knew it. It wasn't going to be long before they were all over one another for bigger shares of what was left. As one of those who still had things to lose, he didn't want to see it get to that point.

"That's it, then," he said. "Let's go get as many big trucks in here as we can that are in good shape. We'll inventory what we have and get them loaded. We can work in shifts. When we're nearly ready to go, we can take a couple of bulldozers out and clear the road up to the west pass."

Jessup had been in construction, he knew he could get the road cleared. Dan could get the young men and the boys motivated to guard their perimeter, at least for a while. Tish would be the one to get the supplies gathered and the trucks loaded. It wasn't any sort of a dream team for survival, but they'd get by.

"Let's get to it," he said.

They milled about a few minutes longer, and then Dan grabbed Jack and Lonnie and headed out. Jessup sent Brian Winslow back for his boy Michael. Both men had worked with

Jessup before things had gone to hell, and both knew their way around heavy equipment. Not much maintenance had been done recently, and it might take them some time to get what they needed fueled and on their way to clear the road.

It was good to have a purpose; it'd been too long.

———

In the end it took a week. Jack Cooper didn't show up for work the second day of the second week, and others had to fill in. Lonnie said it was something his brother had eaten, but there was a glint of emotion in the boy's eyes that made Jessup's stomach twitch. Probably Jack was just too damned lazy for any hard work, but there was no way to tell. Lonnie wasn't talking, and there was too much to do to worry about it.

They lost a half day when Lonnie got a front loader stuck trying to dislodge a fallen tree. He hadn't wanted to bring the boy, but Dan didn't trust him on patrol. No reason given, but Lonnie's weapon had been taken, and Jessup wasn't about to let a healthy body go to waste. It was a mistake.

When Jessup confronted him, it was hard to read the reaction. Lonnie remained distracted, staring off first into town, then into the mountains. He nodded at all the right times, and he really did seem upset that he'd wrecked the front loader, but something was off.

"Jack still sick?" Jessup asked at last. "It's been days now. Do we need to get Tish over to look at him?"

"No!"

Lonnie's answer was too loud, and too quick. Jessup started at him and frowned.

"What's going on with him, Lonnie? Is he sick at all?"

The boy managed a half-assed glare. "He's sick as a dog–some kind of stomach flu. He's had it before–we both have. It'll pass."

When Jessup didn't relent on his stare, the boy added, "He should be up and around by tomorrow, next day at the latest. I got some oatmeal into him this morning."

"We'll reach the highway late tomorrow afternoon. After that, time will be short. If he's getting better, you'll want to be keeping him on his feet and active. Road can be rough."

Lonnie's already pale face grew momentarily slack. He seemed on the verge of saying something, and then bit it back.

"He'll be ready."

Jessup nodded.

"I'm sorry about the front loader."

Jessup shook his head. He was already thinking about the last twelve cans of beer he and Mae had been saving.

"We won't need it. We're leaving, remember? Get some rest."

As the boy walked away toward town, Jessup leaned on the back tire of a big Caterpillar Bulldozer and watched him go. He walked too fast, and he looked around nervously as he went. Jessup spat into the dirt. Something was going on, but he couldn't put a finger on it. He might ask Dan, if he saw him.

He turned back to the road and scanned the rim of the cliff carefully. Sweat made him blink, and the sun was starting to drop toward the horizon. He didn't see anyone moving. He knew Dan, or Dan's people, were out there, but he didn't see them either. Suddenly, thinking about the ruined country lying around them, the dead, the crumbling cities, the poisoned water and ruined air, he felt very alone. A sudden chill made him push off the Cat, and he started down toward town, thinking maybe he understood why Lonnie had walked like the Devil was on his trail.

The last day was rougher than Jessup had anticipated. It was hot, and they worked steadily. He was determined to reach the rim. Wiley, which had been his rock through the months since the attack, seemed big, and empty, full of shadows. He just wanted it over with–the road clear, and the group on the road. If they had things to do–work to concentrate on–they should be all right. That's what he told himself.

It wasn't until nearly six that the final bit of debris was shoved aside. The road beyond, a short feeder road to the freeway, was as good as clear, and he decided they could navigate around what little stood in their way. Cars and buses abandoned. Trucks turned on their sides and garbage lining the ditches. The men and women who'd driven them were long gone. Some had come to Wiley for a time, but they always left. They drifted. They took cars, gas, some took bikes and motorcycles, but they all went. Their lives were in other places– probably blown to hell, or sick with radiation, but still they went.

Jessup stared off into the distance, shading his eyes with one hand. Nothing moved, and after a moment he turned back and started down the hill. He drove the bulldozer. The other equipment had moved ahead of him. He needed to get his rig off the road, and they'd be able to move out–slowly–and start the search for civilization beyond the valley. The search for something that still mattered, and for enough to keep them all busy enough to prevent insanity.

Jessup didn't hear the truck's motor at first over the drone of the bulldozer. As he reached the bottom of the road and slowly rolled off the pavement, a sleek yellow pickup roared out of a side street, skidded, and headed straight at him. Jessup cursed and gunned the big machine's engine. The pickup shot past. He stared in shock.

There were three people in the front of the truck. The bed was loaded and tied down with a large blue tarp. The driver's face was clear. Jack Cooper stared at him with bright eyes and a maniacal twist to his lip.

Beside him, hanging on and looking scared as hell was Lonnie, but Jessup barely noticed. As the truck shot past him, kicking up gravel, he saw the third face, staring out at him through the dusty windshield. It was Mae. Her eyes were as wide as saucers, and she was trying to scream, but her mouth was sealed with duct tape. He thought her arms were tied behind her, but he didn't get a long enough look to be sure. He dove off the bulldozer and started after the truck on foot, but it was only seconds before the pickup shot over the rim he'd just cleared, and disappeared from sight.

Jessup stood and stared after them, then screamed in frustration and anger and took off for his home at a run. He knew his truck was no match for the Cooper's pickup, but the freeway wasn't a hundred percent clear, and he'd been driving a hell of a lot longer than Jack. He didn't think about food, or water. He didn't think about anything but his truck, his gun, and Mae.

He turned the corner and saw his home, what had been his home, and he stopped. It looked as if the front wall had been blown off...maybe it had. His truck was canted over on its side, its windows smashed. Where his front door had been there was just a hole in the wall. Smoke curled out from the interior. Jessup saw Dan standing in front of the structure, waiting.

"Dan," Jessup screamed. "They got Mae."

Dan nodded. He turned and stared into the ruined home. Jessup kept running.

"Did you hear me? I have to go after them. My truck..."

Dan didn't turn around, and Jessup slowed slightly. Dan glanced at him.

"You can't catch them," he said matter-of-factly. "They're gone."

"They got Mae," Jessup repeated.

Dan nodded again. "They did."

He turned back toward the city and scanned the streets.

"We need to get moving early tomorrow," he said, not meeting Jessup's gaze. "Trucks are loaded, and Tish has everything organized."

Jessup grabbed his friend by the shoulder and spun him around.

"Are you not hearing me? They blew up my house. They took my wife. I have to go after them."

"No," Dan said evenly, "you don't. You know you don't. They're long gone, and if they aren't, we'll find them on the road. Probably the others will get them–they aren't too smart." Dan hesitated, and then added, "I'm sorry about Mae. You know you can't go after them though. Things have changed, Jess, and not for the better. We don't have much, but we need to keep it together. We're pulling out in the morning."

Jessup stared at his house. Tears ran down his cheeks. He might have stood there like that until the sun rose the next morning, but at that moment, something inside ignited, and flames shot out the windows and licked at the doorframe. Dan dropped at the first sound, but Jessup was caught by the blast. The concussion lifted him and tossed him back like a rag doll. He saw red, and then the dark, star-filled sky, and then he hit. Hard. After that, he saw nothing.

The next morning, they rolled out of Wiley. There were three large trucks, and towed behind the last was a Jeep. Also included in the convoy was the tanker truck that had been in town to fill the gas station's tanks when the world turned on its side. They'd pumped it full, and Dan was up behind the wheel. He carried a shotgun across his lap.

Jessup watched the houses pass from the passenger side of the truck Tish was driving. She'd tended his wounds, and despite a pounding headache, he'd recovered well enough. He was shaky, and he felt as if he'd swallowed a ball of barbed wire, but he knew Dan was right. They passed the ruined frame of his home, and he closed his eyes. He tried to picture things the way they'd been, but all he saw was Jack's leering stare, and the terrified, empty expression he'd last seen on Mae's face.

As he closed his eyes, he couldn't help but wonder if she'd let them in.

Cuttlefish Squeezings

A Three Word Challenge Poem

Cuttlefish / Sardonic / Moss

Her sardonic smile split
Lips red as sunset fire and thin
So thin, how to begin?
They bled…bitten through
A thousand times,
Punctuating epithets and rhymes
With pain,
Drawing up from swampy graves
Drenched in moss and mired in time
Black plantations and
Forgotten tombs,
Her pages dripp with ink so black
Cuttlefish squeezings,
Like bitter juice
scratched in eldritch patience

and dried on vellum skin.

One Off From Prime

The walls of the shelter were dingy and gray. The paper was white, or had been white. Too many hours stuffed in the bottom of Angus' bag had dampened the sheets and marred their sheen. Most of the pages were empty, windows and doors to places the words hadn't yet taken him; even doors need a new coat of paint now and then–a hinge, or a knob replaced. Angus' paper, as his mind, remained unhinged and without knobs or slots, collecting flecks of dust and smears of sweat and blood.

He wasn't alone in the room, but he might as well have been. Angus stood adrift in a whirling miasma of images and words so thick they obscured the bland walls and walking, talking worlds that orbited him.

A thin, wisp of a woman sidled up sneakily and glanced sidelong into Angus' vacant eyes. She eased along the table, trailed her bony fingers over its surface and watched with bird-like intensity for any reaction. Angus didn't flinch. The woman's dry, pale lips curled into a cruel grin. Like a striking snake her hand darted past the sheet of paper Angus held flat on the table and gripped the strap of his old, green duffle bag.

There was a blur of motion, and the woman screamed. Between her fingers, gouged into the surface of the table and quivering, stood Angus' pen. It didn't touch her skin, but it prevented the sliding of the duffle across the table. The plastic shaft of the pen was shattered, but the inner plastic tube and the ballpoint were intact, quivering from the impact.

Without a word, Angus worked it free of the table. The woman fluttered back and away. She sputtered words that died in strangled bleats of sound and a yellow mist of spittle. Angus paid no more attention to her departure than he had to her approach. He stared at the paper in front of him and willed the words to stop spinning and sort themselves. He had to capture them and bind them to the paper to get them out from in front of his eyes and behind his ears.

He thought–no, he knew–that there was one word among them that could set him free, if only he could unravel the rest and place it properly. He vaguely remembered others who had once helped with the placement, but though he knew there had been three, he couldn't recall names or faces.

None of those around him saw the words. They saw a thin, emaciated man of thirty or so years with thick black hair that dropped over wide, narrow shoulders, their strength belied by thin, protruding shoulder blades. They saw wide eyes that stared at everything except what was directly in front of them and long, slender fingers perpetually wrapped around a pen, or a pencil, or a paintbrush.

One time the counselors had found Angus in the alley behind the shelter with a piece of charcoal in his hand. He'd covered half the back wall with a single long, rambling sentence.

A young woman, thinner still than the insectile Angus, had stood midway along the wall, reading. Her slender, beak-like nose had pressed so close to the wall that its tip was black from accidental encounters with charcoal and brick. Her hands had been filthy from trailing along behind. She'd worn thick cats-eye glasses that slid down her nose and had to be pressed back into service every few minutes. This action, over the course of her reading, had streaked her face with more of the charcoal.

When the counselors had led the two back inside she'd looked ready for a combat raid, camouflaged and intense. Angus, as usual, had looked confused and on the verge of saying something he couldn't quite remember. He'd written it down, but she'd caused it to blur. She'd taken the words into her pores or her skin and the ridges of her fingers. The counselors took the charcoal, and by the time anyone thought to try and read what Angus had written, the words had faded and smudged.

Angus didn't remember the wall. He remembered that there had been words, but not what they'd been. He remembered the young woman's face. He remembered the dark swatches of charcoal embedded in the pores of her skin. He remembered her expression, and her eyes. He'd wanted to reach out, brush his fingers over her cheeks and drag the black, dusty smudges back into the proper order. He'd memorized her features in an instant and imagined them covered in letters, the words merging to one long statement encompassing everything he was unable to say. He thought she was more beautiful without the words, but had no way to be certain.

Now he stared at the blank paper, clutched the shattered pen and tried to bring her face into focus and transfer it to the page. He imagined the lines of letters, like soldiers, or the bricks on a wall. His lips moved, but before he could record the wispy letters in their proper order they slipped away and new ones took their places, always a step ahead. His hand trembled, but he didn't touch the pen to the paper.

The girl sat in the corner of the room, huddled in a severe chair of hard wooden slats. She clutched her knees to her chest and her chin rested between them. She gazed in unwavering concentration at Angus' profile. She saw the paper clearly, and the pen. She knew the tremble in his hand and the nervous shake of his head. She'd seen both so many times they'd become a part of her.

She didn't have to huddle in the shelter. She didn't have to watch this skinny man stare at his paper and chase the words flitting through his head. She had a home, and a name, a family who wondered where she had gone, and friends–acquaintances, really–who noted the empty spaces she would have filled in their own small worlds. But none of that was real. They knew the thin, wispy shell of her, but her connection to Angus was much deeper. Given time, she'd fade from their minds as surely as Angus' words had faded from the alley wall.

Angus knew she was there. He felt her. He sat, and he tried to imagine the lines of her face on his paper, but he refused to turn and watch her watching him because it was no good. The face smudged with charcoal had been cleaned. The words, if they were still there, were hidden too deeply for him to recapture. If he looked at her now, the earlier image of her would dissolve, and be lost. He would still have her eyes, of course, and that was a temptation. They were eyes that had watched him without guile, and without judgment. They were hungry eyes as eager to see him find the order in the words, or behind them, as he was to provide it. They had seen the words, if only for a few intense moments.

Others watched, as well, but not for long, and not with much interest. An old Italian man in a faded army uniform shirt covered in colorful patches shuffled by. He looked like an ancient, rotting parody of a boy scout. He wore two pairs of pants and had a variety of odd items tied to his belt, protruding from his pockets, and slung about his neck. His hair, which would have been a fine blend of white and gray had he bathed, was dark and greasy and clung to his liver-spotted scalp in sparse patches. The man glanced over Angus' shoulder at the blank page and snorted.

"Shouldn't write it down," he said. His voice was weak and formed of shrill, reedy tones that shattered in the air like icicles. "They'll read it. They'll know. Never write it down."

Then he shuffled off with his hands covering his pockets as if afraid the things he carried would leap out and escape. Angus didn't look up. He sat with his hand hovering over the page expectantly.

Some spoke as they passed. Some stared at the paper, or at the back of his head. Some made faces behind his back and then walked on. A tall black man walked around to the far side of the table, directly across from Angus and stared down at the point where the pen had slammed into the tabletop. His lips moved constantly. Now and then his shoulder dipped, or he shuffled his feet. His hips swayed to music no one heard.

He leaned in and inspected the table. A small pile of dust and shattered plastic circled the point where Angus had slammed his pen into the wood. The black man studied it. He cocked his head, checking perspective, and then seated himself in a chair. Angus didn't look up. The black man reached into his pocket and pulled out a small pouch. From this he extracted a razor blade. The cold steel glittered like fire in the dim light, catching stray flickers from the bare, yellowed overhead bulb that illumined the room. It was the kind of blade used by artists and carpenters, braced on one edge with a rounded shield to protect the fingers.

The man's hand darted out. He smacked the blade loudly on the table and drew it toward himself. The razor swept the plastic shards and dust across the surface, his fingers nimbly dropping and dragging, scooping the remnants into a pile. He was careful and he missed nothing. When he had it all in a heap in front of him, he raised the blade and chopped at the pile.

Everyone in the room except Angus, and the girl, looked up sharply. The man brought the blade up, and down, up and down; his fingers flew and quickly pulverized the larger shards of plastic, cutting them to dust, reshaping the mound, and cutting again, each run through making a finer powder. No one in the room spoke. The black man's lips never stopped moving, but if he spoke, there was no sound to accompany it, and if he was answered it was not from anyone nearby.

When the plastic was reduced to glittering dust, the man stopped and studied it. He drew the blade through the center, split the pile, and then split those piles. He cocked his head again. His shoulder dipped. He squinted with one eye and shivered, as if a particularly beautiful rhythm had rippled through his long, lanky body. The ripple ended at his fingers and they danced.

When he was done, there were six lines on the tabletop. Three of them were broken lines. Each of the six lines was of equal length; all were perfectly parallel with one another. The man carefully returned his blade to its pouch, rose from his chair, and did a careful quickstep in place, dropping his hip and throwing his hand out to one side. He turned and walked away.

Angus looked up. The girl rose, came to stand beside him, and stared down at the lines.

Behind them, the door to the room opened and the world poured in. The sudden shift in air pressure sent the dust whirling off the table and away, erasing the trigram.

A voice called out, "Angus Griswold?"

The room they put him in was white-walled. The table he sat at was covered in white Formica. There were windows, but they were the kind that was only transparent in one direction. On his side, they were mirrors. Angus stared at one for a long time, intrigued by the lines of his own face staring back at him. He wondered briefly if, on the far side of that mirror, the words made sense. He had the odd sensation that he recognized himself, and then it was gone.

They had the girl too. She was in another room. He felt her presence, though he hadn't seen her since being closed off. He hadn't seen anyone, in fact, since a very stiff-backed young man in a white jacket had brought him a white cup. He half-expected it to be filled with milk in the colorless void, but it was coffee. Angus loved coffee, but he hadn't touched it. He wasn't afraid of being poisoned, he was concentrating. The room was white, but the coffee was dark, like the words, and it distracted him. He watched the white walls and daydreamed that ink might sweat out through hidden pores in their surface and flow into words and phrases.

In another room, not so bright, and not so white, the girl sat. On the desk in front of her was the remnant of a day planner. The spine had cracked and worn away and the pages were loose. She kept them bound in a pair of large rubber bands she'd stolen from the post office.

She glanced up as the door to the room opened. A tall black man in a dark suit entered, closed the door behind him, and crossed to the far side of the desk. He took a seat and placed a folder in front of her. His eyes were dark brown, so dark they seemed black, and she saw that the cuticles of his fingers were meticulously groomed. He steepled his fingers.

She glanced up at him. He wore thick framed glasses. The wrinkles at the corners of his eyes looked as though they might be accustomed to humor, but in that moment his gaze was flat and serious.

"Why am I here?" she asked.

"I think you know the answer to that." He replied. "I am Mr. Johnson. You don't know me, but I believe you are very familiar with a former associate of mine, Mr. Griswold. You may also have heard of my employer, Mr. King."

"I don't know anyone named Griswold," she said.

"His first name is Angus."

She didn't answer.

"Do you have any idea what Angus did when he worked for us, Miss Prine?"

Her head jerked up. She had not known that they were so close to knowing her name. She smiled, but she tucked her head to hide it, and she didn't answer.

"That's unfortunate. It seems that Mr. Griswold has also forgotten."

Johnson fell silent for a moment, then flipped open the folder on the desk.

"Angus Griswold was a financial analyst. He was very good at his job. Possibly too good. He and his team had the task of scanning pages and pages of computer data and...anticipating."

"Anticipating?"

"I think that's the best way to word it. Angus had a way of seeing a very large amount of data at once. This ability of his allowed him to anticipate trends, predict problems, and circumvent inefficiency. One thing my company loathes beyond all else, Ms. Prine, is inefficiency."

"I don't…"

A sharp jangle of sound cut off his reply. Johnson slid a thin cell phone from his pocket.

"Yes?"

She watched his face, but his expression never changed.

"You're sure," Johnson said. "Four hours, then? I see."

He flipped the phone closed and turned back to her.

"There's not much time. Mr. Griswold has been working on something very important for a very long time. He indicated to us that he'd discovered something big–something profound. That knowledge could prevent a large-scale disaster from taking place, and Mr. King is very interested in obtaining it. Mr. Griswold told us the nature of the disaster, and even gave us a rough idea of when it might take place. Unfortunately, we did not immediately see the importance of what he told us, and at that point his behavior had become–unstable. The file he left behind is incomplete. The single data point he failed to mention before disappearing into the streets was how to stop it."

"He doesn't know," she said. "He's been trying to figure it out. He believes that he will be able to write it down."

"How do you know?"

"He wrote it on the wall. I read it. It was too much to take in at a single reading, and they came and took us away. The words were gone, smudged and ruined. I had them…but they slipped away."

"Do you remember?"

"No. Not all of it. I've written some of it down, but it's not perfect. There was a design."

"Design?"

"Six lines. It was a trigram, like in the I Ching. I drew it."

She fumbled at her ruined day planner. Her hands shook, and she had trouble spreading the pages. When she found it, she slid it free and turned it to face Johnson.

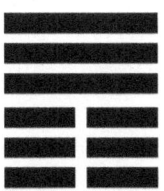

"What is it?" Johnson asked.

"It's a Hexagram. I looked it up at the library. It means Obstruction. Stagnation."

"He wrote this?"

She shook her head. "No. He caused it."

Johnson stared at her a long moment, then made some unspoken decision.

"You have to help us. There is not time to explain the entirety of what is at stake, so I will be brief. I believe that you understand a lot more than you let on."

She held her silence.

"If we do not find the answers we seek, a few tiny calculations in a very large algorithm will return bad data. At first, no one will see. It won't even matter. Over time, the errors will multiply. There is a critical point after which, even if we were to discover the original error, nothing we could do would halt its progress. That error is embedded deep in the database behind the world's largest finance and credit system."

"What can one tiny error do?"

"One error is incorporated in a thousand calculations, the results of which will fuel a hundred thousand more. The integrity of the data will be compromised within minutes. When the world gets the first hint that we do not have control of the system–that their millions of dollars are suddenly in question without even a good direction to point their finger, there will be anarchy. Mr. King believes that within only a few moments, automatic fail-safes and security protocols will shut down everything."

"Everything?" she asked. "Surely there are backups? Contingencies?"

"Also corrupt. We do not believe we will be able to pinpoint the entry point of the error. We believe it is possible that Mr. Griswold can, or already has and has forgotten. We believe, in fact, that he's been trying to put what he already knows in words that others can understand. Even if we found the error and returned the system to its current state it's likely trust and confidence will have eroded sufficiently by that time to cause worldwide panic."

"Where is he?" she asked.

"He is safe, for the moment. As safe as any of us can really be."

She stared at Johnson for a long moment.

"I need to see him."

"Why?"

"He needs to remember. He believes that I can help. He won't look at me, and I think this is because, in his mind, he will either find what he is looking for in the lines of my face, or will find that it is lost forever, and he's afraid."

"I see," Johnson said. "We will give him time, then. The room we put him in is one giant blank canvas. The walls are made of dry-erase white board. The windows are mirrors. The table is white, the floor is white. Soon he will be given markers. We have, at the best estimate of those who have an inkling of what Mr. Griswold has seen, about four hours. If he can't write it down before then; if we get so close to the deadline that there is no hope, I will take you to him. You may be that hope."

She continued to stare at him. Johnson remained unruffled. "Coffee?" he asked.

She nodded, and then looked away, trying to see through the walls to where Angus was seated. She had visions of her own, had been having them since the first time she laid eyes on him so very long before. In her dreams, the angels warned of fire. They warned of destruction. Each of them wore a very large, ticking clock on a golden chain, and the clocks were winding down. In those dreams, men worshiped idols made of shifting symbols and scrolling numbers, falling away to dust.

Johnson slipped out of the room without a sound. The door closed behind him and she stared at it, just for a moment. He had not hesitated, or fumbled with the knob, but she knew it was locked. Less than four hours. The room didn't even have a clock.

Johnson stood behind a row of three chairs. The chairs faced a bank of huge monitors across which columns and patterns of numbers shifted and scrolled. Each screen was divided into terminal windows, and different events triggered flashes of color. In the chairs, a young Asian woman, an old gray-haired man, and a boy of about sixteen sat. On the backs of their chairs, the names Meshe, Shad, and Abe had been scrawled across white nametags. They watched the scrolling numbers, working keyboards, trackballs and a bank of peripheral controls without once glancing away from the screen.

Johnson wanted to question them, but he knew that either they would ignore him, as per their instructions, or he'd likely cause a new set of problems by his interference. When Angus had worked with them, there'd been a fourth chair. Mr. King had removed it when the prodigal walked out.

Johnson watched the numbers for a moment, but they meant little to him. When they had been sifted down to spreadsheets and balanced equations, he'd understand them well enough. In their current raw state, it was beyond his ability. That was fine–it wasn't his job. His job was to be certain that the numbers did balance. In the upper levels of the company, they joked that every transaction since the beginning of time flowed across those screens–that the Templars had kept records, and the Egyptians had been meticulous.

The woman, Meshe, gasped suddenly. She didn't stop working her controls, and she didn't look away from the screen, but he knew that she'd caught something. Her distress passed, and he knew it couldn't be what Angus had seen. These three were very good. There had once been more than two dozen "watchers" working in shifts, and they had all been good. None of them had borne Angus' singular gift–or his neuroses. Now there were only three, and though Angus had spoken to them before leaving, none of them could find the fault, though they would no doubt remain vigilant.

Johnson turned away and left the room as silently as he'd entered. He headed down a brightly lit hall and entered through the glass doors of the office at the far end. An elderly man, grey at the temples glanced up from where he'd been scouring reports on his desk.

"What has he said?" the man asked.

"Nothing. He's confused and barely coherent. The girl isn't much better. I think it's time to put them together and see what comes of it."

"It's our last shot. If they can't get it back in time…"

"I know," Johnson said. "Don't think I haven't considered walking out, buying a bunker in a survivalist camp and stocking up. We haven't got much time. For all we know we don't have any time at all. We have to try it now."

"Take her in," the man said.

Johnson turned, hesitated, and looked back.

"It's been good working with you, Ezekiel."

The older man smiled. It was a fleeting expression that looked lost in the patchwork of stress-fractures that made up his face. Then he turned back to the papers, and Johnson slipped into the hallway, closing the door quietly behind him.

———

When the door opened, Angus didn't look up. The girl entered, and the door closed behind her. She sat opposite him at the table. He stared at the white surface, refusing to meet her gaze.

"You wrote it down once," she said. "In the alley. You wrote it down, and it was all there."

Angus twitched, but did not look up.

"I knew you'd get it. I knew you'd find the words. It's why I watched, and why I read."

"They're gone." Angus said.

She shook her head. She rose, circled the table, and stood directly beside him, but still he did not look up. She reached out and stroked his cheek. He didn't pull back, but she felt the inner struggle. He quivered as if unable to decide whether to press into her fingers, or to lean away.

"The words are not gone. If they were gone, you'd be at rest. They are there, buzzing and crackling with energy, and you need them to stop. We both need that. The world needs that. You started it, and only you can finish it. It's up to you."

She stepped behind his chair, pulled it gently away from the table, then slid around and straddled him. With one hand on each cheek she raised is head until he stared directly at her.

"It's time," she said.

Angus shivered, but he didn't look away. She leaned closer, and her features blurred. At the end, he saw her lips, red and moist, and crisscrossed with tiny veins that shifted and rearranged. They kissed and those crooked, wretched lines clarified. Angus pulled back, just for an instant, but she held him fast.

His mind flooded with memories. Lines of figures flashed past on mental monitors so fast it should have been dizzying, but he already knew them. He felt each ripple and saw the tiny bugs nibbling away at the heart of the pattern.

He was vaguely aware when she began stroking her hips up and down. He rose to meet her and wrapped her in his arms. He was so close. He had walked so long in a world that buzzed and whirled that the clarity was painful. The haze beckoned. He itched to hold his pencils, or a piece of chalk. The white walls streamed with row after row of symbols and numbers and he wanted to fill them in and trap them. He felt her unbutton his shirt and then the hot touch of her flesh and then…he let them go.

Johnson and Ezekiel stood before a huge video monitor. On the screen, Angus stood, disheveled and coated in sweat, before one of the white walls. He held a dry-erase marker in his hand, poised. Behind him, the woman lay back across the table, spent. It was difficult not to stare at her; something in the aspect of her pose gave her a sensuality her street-urchin attire and schizophrenic actions had hidden. She did not look at Angus, but instead stared back at them through the monitor, as if well aware her naked flesh was on camera and reveling in the attention.

"My God," Ezekiel said. "Who is she?"

"You know who she is. You know what she is. What neither of us knew was how profoundly *real* she would turn out to be."

"She calls herself Prine?" Ezekiel asked absently.

"I think we may have been mistaken. It sounded like Prine, and we have assumed that to be correct, but upon closer examination of the original document, I believe she is called…Prime."

"It's her last name?"

"It's her only name."

"My God."

"Not exactly, but…wait! He's writing."

On the screen Angus reached out with the marker. He started drawing horizontal lines. After only a few seconds work the hexagram was complete. "Obstruction". He stared at it, and then turned.

"There is no new flaw in the numbers," he says.

It's not a question, but it's directed to the girl."

"Of course not. There is only the one flaw. You knew this once."

"I know it again," he said.

He dropped the marker on the floor and it rolled under the table. He walked to the table and lifted her to a sitting position. She smiled into his stern gaze. Angus leaned in and kissed her, and then turned toward the cameras.

"Numbers are pure," he said. "The system by which you calculate them is a language, and it is the closest to perfection man may ever come, but there are flaws. There have always been flaws. You have built a world on numbers, filled in the cracks when the foundations shifted, and applied new paint, but the central flaw was always there. It's eaten at the foundations since the first dollar was saved and reinvested. It's the root cause of all the tiny cracks I patched for you, and the thousands more rising to the surface."

"Tell them about Schrödinger's Cat," she said.

He turned and frowned at her, and then the frown cracked into a crooked smile.

Ezekiel turned and started to ask Johnson a question, but Johnson held up a hand. He focused intently on Angus.

"I spent my life looking for flaws in the perfection of the data. No matter how many times I found and fixed a problem, the imperfection screamed at me, and I had to go on. All I was doing was plugging holes in a sinking ship. There was never any perfection to mar, only a crumbling façade."

Johnson stepped back from the monitor. Behind him a red light began flashing slowly, and then another. Alarms sounded. Ezekiel turned and glanced at them. He touched Johnson on the shoulder, but Johnson shrugged him off.

"It's too late, Ezekiel," he said.

Johnson reached out and pressed a button. He leaned down and spoke into a microphone on the desk beside the monitor.

"Angus," he said.

Angus turned and looked directly into the camera.

"I cannot speak to you," he said. "I have a message for Ezekiel."

The old man stood very still. Johnson turned to stare at him, and then pressed the microphone button again.

"Ezekiel is here."

"Now is the time, old friend. You must remember. Mr. King and his minions have built this false idol of greed and gold, this mountain of numbers. You know what will happen should it crumble, and yet, the choice remains yours. Worship, or be taken by fire."

"Your name is not Angus," Ezekiel said. His voice was soft, as though he was forcing memories from somewhere deep inside.

"What are you talking about?" Johnson said. He shook Ezekiel hard. "What do you mean he isn't Angus? Who is he?"

"Call the main office," Ezekiel said, ignoring the question. Get Nebbu...get Mr. King on the line. Tell him...tell him that we choose the fire."

The blinking lights and alarms lit the wall behind them like a holiday celebration. Johnson ignored them. He stared at Ezekiel, and then turned back to where Angus still stared through the camera and into his soul.

"Who are you?" Johnson asked. "Who, in God's name, are you?"

"Names are only patterns," Angus replied. Then he smiled. "I am many, and I am one. I would tell you that I am the way, the truth, and the light, but she–pointing at the girl–would tell you I am Hermes, or Mithras, or Odin, and she cannot lie. It does not matter who I am. What matters, and what has always mattered, is who *you* are, and what you will become.

"The numbers have failed. In the beginning, there was the word–and that is all there has ever been. Plurality is divisive. Heaven isn't a chord; it's a single, pure note. Go, and learn to sing."

The monitor went dark. Power in the building flickered, and then dropped. For a long moment auxiliary power tried to kick in and bring it back to life–and then that too died. Ezekiel had gone. Johnson sifted through unfamiliar memories. He thought of the three in the other room, staring at blank screens that had been filled with numbers only moments before. He mouthed their names, and almost laughed.

"Shadrach, Meshach, and Abednego," he said softly. How had he not seen?

It didn't matter. Without a backward glance he turned, left the room and the building and walked out into the world. Behind him the monitor blinked to life without external power.

Angus and Prime stood, wrapped in a tight embrace. Dark flecks danced up from the floor, peeled off the walls, and began to whirl. The flecks grew, diving and dancing through the air until they enlarged to numbers, and words, letters and symbols. The cloud whirled faster and darker until the room was obscured by a tangle of dark images and shifting patterns.

And then it was gone. All that remained in the room was a battered spiral notebook and a number two pencil. On the top sheet, the Hexagram symbolizing "Obstruction" had torn down its center. On the streets beyond the building, men and women stepped out into bright sunlight…so bright, it burned.

Loch Ness

That foul Loch Ness shall be no more a cairn,
Nor nightmare for the wives of sturdy men,
Nor used to fright the dickens from the bairn,
No, not a cairn, that hellish pit's a den,
For that most fearsome beastie, sliding deep
Within those darksome keeps of mud and slime
Awaiting only time, a chance to seep,
Up from the gloom and shadows, slowly climb,
Upon the surface, breaking like a wave
To claim as nightmare brethren all who see,
And those unlucky few we cannot save,
Killed, or eaten? Merely ceased to be?
My eyes bear witness to that hideous beast,
And thankful not to be part of its feast...
Attributed to Angus William Griswold–rough translation

Headlines

Harry O'Flanagan stood alone in the center of a field one mile south of Nyxon and watched the wheezing, gasping approach of the old truck impatiently. It was no Chevy, or Ford that chugged over the uneven terrain. Exhaust puffed out of every available pipe and a few unplanned holes. The afternoon sun glinted off bits and pieces of crystal and chrome. There was no single material that comprised frame or body, nor was there a color that could be ascribed to the paint. If any pair of parts had originally been designed to work together, there was no indication of it. Harry noticed none of this; he'd seen the truck plenty of times and long since given up guessing at its secrets. All he cared about at that moment was its cargo and how god-awful slow it was moving. Harry was on a schedule–he had places to go, things to see.

The truck pulled to a stop, gave a final kick and a bang, and died. Steam whistled up and out of the engine in so many places it might have been a metal statue of a wheel of Swiss cheese. The driver's side door opened, and a tall, gaunt man stepped out. He was dressed in jeans so faded they seemed to have no color at all, worn boots that looked too long and narrow, and a green plaid flannel shirt. He stood at least six foot five, and when he'd unfolded and stretched, Harry had to crane his neck and shield his eyes from the sun to meet the newcomer's gaze.

"Afternoon, Cyrus," Harry said. "I was starting to wonder if you'd make it."

Cyrus turned toward the truck and frowned. "Had some trouble loading. It's a big one, Harry. Biggest one yet. Not sure what's going to happen when we let it loose."

Harry followed Cyrus' gaze to the truck, then shrugged.

"Only one way to find out," he said.

Cyrus nodded. He turned back to the truck and leaned in over the seat. When he straightened and stepped back he held a double-barreled shotgun cradled in his arms. The truck shook violently.

"Jesus," Harry said. He stepped back a few feet. His camera dangled from a strap that hung around his neck. He lifted it about as high as his chin.

Cyrus stepped around to the back of the truck. The rear of the vehicle was like a U-Haul designed by Escher. The angles were all wrong, though it was somewhat box-shaped. The rear sported double doors currently held tight by a metal bar that slid across and rested in brackets to either side. There were dents and dings on the metal face of those doors. All of them had been made from the inside out. Some of them looked fresh.

"What in hell is in there," Harry asked.

"Tick," Cyrus said solemnly.

"Tick? You created a freaking mutant tick?"

Before he could comment on how little he thought of this idea, Cyrus kicked the bar loose from the rear doors of the truck and stepped back. They burst open immediately, but nothing rushed forth. Instead, the massive rear end of a huge, slick-skinned creature popped through the opening. It was very still, just for a moment, then there was a horrible scrabbling sound and the truck started shaking again.

"Jesus, Cyrus, how the hell did it get *in* there?"

"Wasn't so big then," Cyrus explained, keeping the shotgun steady, the barrel leveled at the thing pulling itself free of the truck. "Hadn't fed. Used to be a cow in there too."

Before Harry could form a proper comment the thing freed itself with a loud, wet pop. It reared up, towering a good three feet over Cyrus' lanky frame. It seemed unaware of their presence, sort of shifting up onto the roof of the truck's rear section and rolling from side to side. Harry glanced past it into the truck's interior. A thin, shriveled bundle lay on the floor. Spots of blood flecked the walls.

"We'll want a picture of the cow, too," he said. "It's a great angle."

Cyrus nodded, but he never turned his gaze from the thing on his truck. At the sound of Harry's voice, it lurched up and back, pivoting grotesquely on segmented, many jointed legs. It was bloated, and as it moved, something wet sloshed. Bile rose in Harry's throat, but he squashed it back down and raised his camera.

It was fast. For all its lumbering bulk, the thing moved like lightning once it spotted them. Harry stumbled back with a cry. He heard the muffled roar of the shotgun and saw Cyrus fall beneath the tick. Harry's heel caught on a protruding rock, and he fell too, wind milling one arm and clutching his camera with the other. When he hit the ground, all breath left him. His vision was stolen by an explosion of stars. He fought for clarity, just for a moment. He heard Cyrus call out to him from what seemed like an impossible distance. He thought he should answer, but the wash of darkness tossed the thought aside easily and dragged him into oblivion.

He awoke with a start, turned to the side and retched. His hand flew instinctively up to wave in front of his face, and he heard someone step back with a grunt. Harry blinked, retched again, and then glanced up through tear-streaked eyes.

Cyrus stood over him. The man was so tall that, from his vantage point seated on the ground, Harry thought he looked like a giant. There was something green and glittering in Cyrus' hand, and Harry's thoughts focused. The stench that had invaded his senses had faded somewhat, and he took a chance, shaking his head lightly to clear it. The pain wasn't too bad.

"What the hell is that STINK?" Harry asked.

Cyrus didn't answer. He stoppered the bottle and tucked it into the breast pocket of his flannel shirt. "Best you don't know," he said.

Harry stared at Cyrus. Had the man smiled? In all the time Harry had known the strange, thin man, he'd never seen his expression change.

"What happened," Harry asked. He rolled over and got shakily to his feet. He glanced past Cyrus as his memory returned full force. The rear of the truck was splattered with gore. Thick, red blood mixed with some sort of mucous clung like a crimson tarp to the rough surface of the field. The tick's carcass lay behind the truck, feet up and twitching slightly, but it was only about half the size it had been when Harry fell. He frowned.

"Damn," he said.

"You get any shots of it?" Cyrus asked.

Harry glanced down at his camera dubiously. "I'm not sure. Maybe. We'll take some more now. It's still a damned big one, and with that deflated cow…"

He already had the headline fixed in his mind. "Farmer Bags giant Bloodsucker." As usual, before he'd even stepped forward and begun posing Cyrus and the dead monstrosity for his photographs, the words of the story itself formed and embedded themselves in his brain; by the time he sat down to type he'd be doing no more than transcribing a finished product.

"Sorry about the mess," Cyrus said. He walked straight through the red mess toward the truck, and Harry shuddered.

"Damn," he muttered.

When they were done with the shoot, and Cyrus had kicked, shoved, and prodded the carcass of the tick into the rear of his vehicle and sealed it away, Harry shook the man's hand.

"It'll make a dandy cover," Harry said. "Just dandy. You let me know if you get something new or outstanding."

"Of course," Cyrus said, folding himself into the odd driver's seat of his truck. "I've always got something ...in progress."

"I'll be in town a few days," Harry said, speaking before Cyrus could fire up the belching, steam-spitting beast. "I'm looking for Danny. You seen him? I got a message to call him, but no one answers. Really could use something from him this time out–the fan mail is piling up. America can't get enough of the Rat Boy."

Cyrus shook his head slowly. "Not this week," he said. "He brought me some..." The man hesitated, and then shrugged. "He brought me some supplies last weekend. Saturday. Haven't seen or heard from him since. He was staying at The Plaza."

Harry nodded. "Thanks. I'll see if I can find him."

Cyrus started the truck without another word, and moments later he headed back across the field, leaving clouds and a raucous roar in his wake. Harry watched until the truck was halfway across the field, and then turned back toward the line of trees behind him that masked the road into Nyxon. His car was there, an old Dodge Dart closing in on 250,000 miles and looking every inch of it. He really needed a new car. A new job, life, and a dose of sanity wouldn't hurt. He tucked the camera into its weather-beaten case, climbed in and headed for town.

———

The Plaza looked pretty ordinary by day, and after the fracas with Cyrus and his pet, Harry was glad to see it. He turned into the horseshoe shaped drive and parked outside the chrome-framed glass doors. He left the Dart where it was, took his battered overnight bag, camera case, and laptop with him, and headed for the desk. Most of the hotel's staff was nocturnal; he didn't expect his car would cause any major traffic difficulties in the time it took to get a room.

He was right. Twenty minutes later he had the old-fashioned skeleton key in his pocket, the Dodge was tucked away in the parking garage beneath the building, and Harry was planted securely in a thickly padded leather chair. He had the laptop open on an old, ornate roll-top desk, the cursor blinking halfway down a page of text. He'd typed feverishly for the first ten minutes he was in the room, wanting to make sure he captured the story about the giant tick just as he'd imagined it.

It seemed that a farmer, Cyrus, had been plowing his field early in the morning and had come across the thing sucking the life from one of his cows. Being ready for anything, he'd had a shotgun strapped to the back of his tractor, and before the thing could turn on him, he'd bagged it. Harry had already downloaded the pictures, and was pleasantly surprised to find he'd managed to snap off a good shot of the monster rearing up and spinning, just he'd fallen over and missed the whole show. It would make a good two-page spread backdrop for the article, and the shot of Cyrus, standing over the drained cow, shotgun in one hand and dead tick in the other by its scruff would, as Cyrus had observed, "make a dandy cover."

It was a good day's work, but it wasn't Harry's purpose in Nyxon. The cover story was gravy this time out. What Harry needed was the next installment in his greatest creation–the continuing adventures of "Rat Boy," the boy with the face of a rat. He'd been writing the stories for years, ever since meeting Danny the very week he discovered the city of Nyxon, and they were one of the staples of his paper's popularity. Every month or so, Rat Boy would take on some terrorist world leader, or negotiate a treaty with aliens. Harry scripted the adventure, Danny acted out the part, posed for pictures, collected a nice stipend for his trouble, and the world got their laughs.

This time out Harry wanted to find something fresh, something totally unexpected that would drive the Rat Boy fans nuts. He'd taken the week off because he knew that he could write while he was in Nyxon and e-mail the files to the paper as easily as he could make them up in his own office. He hoped that the proximity to Danny would provide the necessary inspiration. The last couple of stories had been too formulaic, even for outright fabrications. It was time to push the human rodent envelope.

Harry finished proofreading what he'd just written, changed a couple of words, then rattled off another rapid-fire paragraph or two. He did a quick word count, found it satisfactory, and hit save. Lights blinked as the story was committed to the laptop's hard drive, and Harry rose. He went to the phone and punched "0" for the Lobby.

"Yes?" The voice on the other end was gravelly, as though the sounds weren't sliding over a human tongue. He suppressed a shiver.

"This is Harry O'Flanagan in room 313. Can I get some hot coffee up here? Also, do you know what room Mr. Weissel is staying in? I need to reach him."

There was a pause, and then the voice returned. "Mr. Weissel is in 242, Mr. O'Flanagan, but I don't believe he's in. He has very particular tastes, and we haven't had an order in almost two days."

Harry stared at the phone. He knew all-too-well what the special nature of Danny's hunger was, but where could the boy be?

"Thanks," he said. "Just send up that coffee, then, and I'll see if I can find him on my own. Room 242, you say?"

"Yes sir," the voice grated. There was a click, a buzz, and when the dial tone returned, he punched the numbers 242 followed by the # sign to connect to Danny's room. They could be wrong. The boy could just be sleeping off a binge of some sort–or maybe he was eating out.

There was nothing. After ten rings he dropped the receiver back into its cradle and returned to the desk. He plugged the laptop into the high-speed Internet connection, ran through the familiar Plaza login routine, and e-mailed the tick story to the paper, along with his photos and instructions for placement and cropping. When he was finished he turned off the computer, closed it, rose, and headed for the door.

He stopped as someone knocked. When he opened the door, he found a very pale young man holding a tray with a fresh pot of coffee, two cups, sugar, and a pair of spoons.

"Room Service," the boy said unnecessarily.

Harry stood aside and watched as the boy, seeming to glide across the carpeted floor, placed the coffee carefully beside the laptop and came back. Harry reached automatically for his wallet, but the boy smiled and slipped out the door.

"No need," he said as he passed.

Harry nodded absently. He'd known, of course, that there was no tipping at the Plaza. He didn't know what had spurred them to such an odd practice, but he hoped the bellboys and waiters were well compensated. He suspected that at least a few of them had a hard time keeping anything solid in their pockets. Not everyone was who or what they seemed in the gray stone walls of the Plaza Hotel.

'Wait," Harry called. "Do you know Danny Weissel? Room 242?"

The boy turned. His grin was a shimmer of sharp white teeth, but there was no menace in the expression.

"Yes, Mr. O'Flanagan," he replied. "He's been with us since last weekend. I haven't seen him today sir."

Harry thanked him, and the boy disappeared down the hall. The coffee was dark, strong, and fresh. Another thing about the plaza. If you came in at four thirty in the morning, the coffee was as fresh as it was at 8:00 AM or 4:30 PM. It was always the same. Perfect. The first cup went down fast, followed by a second. Harry eyed the pot, started to pour a third, then thought better of it. Instead he grabbed the keys to his room, and his car, and slipped out the door.

The hallway was empty, as he'd expected it to be. He reached the elevator without encoutering another soul, and when he stepped out on the second floor, it was the same. He followed the arrows to room 242 and stood outside, staring at it and wishing he had X-ray vision.

He knocked. There was no answer. He knocked again, then, glancing up and down the hall to make sure he was still alone, he pulled out his keys. Along with those to his car, apartment, and various locks back at the office, a small set of lock picks dangled from the ring. He knew he should get them off of there before he got arrested and the wrong questions were asked, but every time he thought about doing it, they came in handy again. Like now.

He wasn't at all certain what would happen when he stuck the bent bit of metal into the keyhole. It wasn't like breaking into an apartment back in San Valencez. Here things were never quite what they seemed. He wouldn't have been at all surprised to hear the lock start screaming, or laughing, as if the lock pick tickled it. Nothing out of the ordinary happened, though; he found the old-fashioned tumblers, twisted the lock pick, and he was in.

The first thing he noticed was that the room was clean. He'd been around Danny enough times to know this was odd. He also noticed that the window was open. A breeze gripped the curtains and sent them dancing to the side. There wasn't much light outside, just a hint of sunlight draining down the sides of the bulidings as it dropped for the night.

Harry stepped to the window and glanced out. That's when he saw it.

Danny's window looked out over a dusty alley. Trash cans, beat up dumpsters, and dingy brick walls stretched in either direction. Near the rear of the alley, almost too far away to see clearly, something long and very low to the ground slunk around a corner. At first glance he thought it must be a snake, and a damned big one. He wondered if Cyrus had accidentally lost control of something. Then he looked more closely.

They were rats. They had formed a line, three or so abreast, and they swarmed forward, their bodies blending and seething en masse. Even after he'd managed to separate them in his mind, it was hard not to see the grisly army of them as a single entity. He'd never seen anything like it.

He glanced down and saw that it was only a short jump to the fire escape. He wondered how long it had been since Danny took that same leap, but it didn't matter. Whatever was drawing those rats around the corner was a story waiting to be written. He considered rushing back to his room for his camera, but thought better of it. He leaned down, patted his ankle, and felt the reassuring weight of the tiny, 22 caliber strapped beneath his sock.

"Christ on a stick," he muttered.

Then he slid his leg over the windowsill, dropped to the metal landing and hurried down the fire escape.

The alley ended in a solid wall, but there was a second, darker alley leading off to the right, and Harry followed it. Twilight had set in, and it was getting increasingly difficult to see the ground in front of him. Images of the swarming rats made his stomach churn and threaten to fill his throat with bile, but he fought it down, trailed his hand over the grimy bricks to keep himself from walking into a wall, or a shadow-drenched dumpster, and moved on.

There was a very dim glow ahead, and where he'd heard only the breeze before, or the distant roar of an engine, he now heard some kind of music. It was difficult to make it out, at first, partly because it was so low in pitch, and partly because his heart was crashing so hard that the subsequent roar in his ears drowned out everything beyond the confines of his head.

The melody was familiar, and it drew the hairs at the back of his neck up like the hackles of a spooked dog. There was no sign of the rats, but with the glowing light becoming brighter at each step, he didn't need to see them. In fact, he prayed fervently *not* to see them again until he was safely out of the alley and back in his room, or even in Danny's.

The smaller alley ended, much like the larger one, and this time the opening to the right was a doorway. It was dark, and he couldn't see if there was a sign or any marking above the door. It was open, and the light he'd seen emanated from within. The music was there, as well. It didn't really seem louder, and yet the sound filled his mind. He fought for concentration. He focused on images of Cyrus, the giant tick, went over story plot lines in his mind and tried humming discordant, irritating versions of Barry Manilow's greatest hits. Anything to disrupt the humming, buzzing drone of the "music" drifting out of that door.

He leaned inside. From the doorway he heard scraping, scratching sounds. He concentrated on these, even though he knew what they must be. He thought about the tiny, furry bodies, long whiskers and beady eyes. He saw long, pink, worm-like tails winding around and over, in and out.

Harry leaned down and pulled his gun free of the ankle holster and slipped through the door. He crouched low and pressed to the nearest wall. The sounds within didn't change at his entrance. The music played on, and the soft, scrabbling footsteps drew no closer. He stook a step forward, then another, feeling along the wall with his left hand and clutching the gun in his right. It felt light, inadequate, and almost silly, and he was afraid the sweat on his palms would cause it to fall free and clatter away into the shadows.

He reached a stair, and very slowly, he descended toward the light. Shadows danced below, and the music–some kind of flute, or pipes–had been joined by a voice. Or had it been there all along? Subtle melodies ran together and blended, scurried and trilled, and to his horror, he realized that the footsteps, the tiny scratches of claws on–what, concrete?–kept time with the song. They were like a rippling percussive rhythm that gave the illusion of holding the sound in place, but was in fact captured within it.

Harry didn't know how he knew this. He didn't even want to think about it, but the thoughts were insidious, invading his mind and pushing away each block of images, or memories, that he placed in their way. The sound wanted him as well. It wanted him to drop to hands and knees, slip into the thronging bodies below, and disappear.

He stopped a few steps from the bottom. He saw a river of rats–an ocean of them–undulating over a floor that might have been another foot down, or ten feet, all fur and bodies, claw and teeth. Their bright eyes were glazed with a dull sheen and they stared mindlessly forward. Harry turned and followed their gaze.

On a raised stone platform a man stood, hunched and curled around a long, wooden flute. The figure didn't look up. Long hair dangled to the floor, where thousands of rats rippled up and over the stone edge, then back down, parting that hair, circling the feet–the legs. And right beside him, head thrown back in ecstasy, moving very slowly, Danny danced.

The boy was enthralled. His eyes had the same unseeing glaze as the rodents beneath him. He moved with a liquid, thoughtless grace, and the sight of it sickened Harry to the core.

Before he could think about what he was doing, he opened his mouth, and he began to sing. At first it was impossible to make out the words. They tangled with the flute, and the skittering, chirruping rats, but he fought it. Harry was a decent Irish tenor, and when he put his lungs behind it, he could belt out drinking songs with the best of them, or do his part to see that the walls of the church needed re-plastering every few years.

He didn't sing a drinking song in that basement room. He didn't sing a hymn. He ignored the musician, and the rats, and stared at his friend, lost in the dance on the stage. Drawing the words and the melody up from his past, he sang them pure, sweet, and as loudly as his lungs would allow.

"Oh Danny Boy, the pipes, the pipes are calling."

There was a rustle among the rats. The musician's elbow, held up high so he could finger the flute more easily, twitched. Harry sang on.

"From glen to glen, and down the mountain side."

The cadence of the rats feet faltered. Danny stopped dancing for a second, shook his head, and when he tried to find the rhythm again, he spun too close to the figure beside him, slapping the flute awkwardly from the man's lips.

The room grew silent. Harry opened his mouth to sing the next verse, but found he could not get the sound to exit his throat. He stared, transfixed, as the creature–he'd thought it was a man, but no man had eyes that wide, or that deep–glared at him. It straightened and took a step closer.

All around them the rats fell into a panic. Without the sound to draw them, their minds sought food, and shelter. They felt the confines of the room and the cool air at their backs, up the stairs to freedom.

Harry had seen too many bad horror movies to just stand there and wait for what came next. He lifted the gun, aimed it at the thing's face, and pulled the trigger.

The echo of the shot crashed thorugh the room, and the rats broke like a wave. Harry heard Danny cry out, heard him scream something from very far away, but he had no time to think about it. He turned, and tried to run back up the stairs. Rats poured aorund his legs, scurried over his hips and up his shirt, dangled from his hair and dashed over him. He staggered, bounced off the wall, climbed another few steps with a curse, and then–overwhelmed, he went down hard. He didn't feel an impact, but the breath was knocked from him, all the same. He tried to call out. He tried to stand, but there was motion all around him. The musky, rat stench choked off his breath. With a croaking groan, he dropped away to darkness.

When he woke, he was seated in his hotel room at the Plaza. Danny sat across from him, watching. Harry started to shake his head, stopped himself just in time as the headache threatened, and instead leaned forward with a groan and cupped his face in his hands.

"You okay?" Danny asked. "I had a hell of a time hauling you back down the alley. Once I got here one of the doormen helped me load you on a luggage cart, and I rolled you to the elevator. I told them you'd had too much to drink, but I don't think they believed me."

"What happened?" Harry asked. "That...thing. What was it?"

"I'm not sure," Danny said. "I have thoughts on the matter, but you'd say I've been reading too many bedtime stories. What in God's name made you waltz in and start bellowing like that? Not that I'm not grateful…"

Harry glanced up. Danny's eyes twinkled. His elongated nose twitched, and one lip curled back, exposing long, gleaming teeth. Harry shivered.

"I need a shower," he said.

Danny laughed. "Don't you want to write the story first?"

Harry stopped and stared.

"While it's fresh in your mind, I mean?" Danny insisted. "I got it started for you right here."

Harry turned to see where his friend was pointing. The laptop stood open on the desktop, and a headline had been typed in bold italic script across the top of a blank page.

"Rat Boy fights off Pied Piper, Saves Irish Reporter from bad Singing Career."

Harry growled and swung, but Danny ducked easily, laughing.

"Have I told you, Danny," he said as he ducked into the bathroom and headed for the shower, "how much I hate rats?"

The Rat Boy laughed, and Harry shivered. In the sound of that laughter, tiny feet skittered, and the distant echo of a long, wooden flute echoed through the shadows.

"Christ on a stick," he muttered. "I have *got* to get a new job."

He stayed under the hot, steaming water a very, very long time, but he thought he'd never rid himself of the fetid, musky smell.

A Poem of Adrian, Gray

Endless spirals,
Ending.
Don Quixote tilting windmills
of loneliness and doubt
against a sunrise backdrop
of hope, sliding relentlessly toward
hopeless.
Solitary fortress
fortified by brief glimpses…
Synapse images of
Dreams half-feared and
Desires molten through
Indecision
To the soul.
Dangling carrot perfection
Slides easily through
timorous groping talons
of self-imposed inadequacy.
Chemically bandaged mind

A POEM OF ADRIAN, GRAY

Driving drained and broken frame,
Buying time/love/nothing
Until the 2000th time
A day is born
and truth and reality
merge - reform- destroy
And twist in endless spirals,
Ending

Wayne's World

(For Wayne Allen Sallee)

I stood alone among the crowds that had gathered outside the prison, watching in ways they could not, and waiting. I was celebrating the death of John Wayne Gacy, but not in the manner that the rest of them were, or not in the manner that I *assumed* they were celebrating. I assumed that they were happy because they felt, foolishly, a bit safer. I assumed, as well, that it was a moment of control for them, a moment in which the evil of the world could be labeled, restrained and in due time erased–wiped out forever.

This latter idea amused me. The "moment of control" theory is one of the prevalent ideas on the motivation of sociopathic killers. It makes sense. It also makes a hell of a mirror for these people to look into if they ever realize why they came down to witness this killing. A sociopathic society?

The control angle is a fantasy. The evil had been diminished not one bit by John's departure from their midst, whatever they

94

might believe. The good guys were not winning. The good guys *couldn't* win. If there were no bad guys, there wouldn't *be* any good guys. Try and explain that to your average citizen, lost in his own little empty-headed world. Try and explain that to anyone, for that matter. Lord knows, *I've* tried.

But that's what it's all about, isn't it? Our own little worlds. Every one of them is different, separate, and distinct. Don't fool yourself into believing otherwise; it's a waste of time. You live in your world, I live in mine, and never the twain shall meet. Period.

Gacy had his world–right up until the end. He had it wrapped tightly around him like a cocoon. They've been studying him for several years now, psychologists, psychiatrists, penal reformists; none of them seem able, or perhaps willing, to see the truth of it. They are trying to analyze an alien landscape by referencing the only thing they have to reference, their *own* little world. That's right. They can't see the light for the trees, so to speak–their own trees.

Sometimes a whole group of worlds seem to align. This is what they call a society. It isn't a true picture, but it lets the weak and unimaginative sleep better at night. When a group of people truly believe that what they see and what their neighbor sees in any given moment are the same, they have deluded themselves. If you give the same coffee, morning paper, and bus-ride to work to twelve different people, the entire scheme of events, actions, and reactions will be absolutely different in each case. Different worlds. Odds are the criteria you use to ascertain this will be based on your own world, so I wouldn't trust your data much on this, either.

Take that newspaper we just mentioned, the one our "control" group read over breakfast. Let's say there's an article covering a killing on the front page–top center, headline in bold print. "Police Apprehend Alleged Kidnapper/Slayer of Three."

This story will not contain facts–not by pure definition. It will contain the impression that society has agreed upon as fact–the majority opinion.

It will not tell you why the killer's world required that these people be abducted and killed. It will not tell you how the police intersected their own reality with that of the criminal and brought him to justice, not really. It will tell you what fits into the pseudo-world of society, and you will believe it, probably. It is the path of least resistance.

John's world is about to come to an end, as he knows it. The others, those who have studied, hated, died, and reviled it–they will never know it at all. You can't enter another man's world. Therein lies the rub, so to speak. Even now, as I pontificate from my own world, I know that every reaction to these words will be different, and that no two people will read them the same way, or with the same outcome. The difference is that I accept this–to a point.

It hit me when I was still a child. Nobody really understood me. I was riding in the car with my mother, watching the houses go by, and it smacked me like a sledge-hammer to the center of the forehead. There were people in each and every one of those houses. Each of them lived a separate life–most of which would never, in any way, interact with my own. Each of them loved, hated, lived and lied–alone. That was fine, as far as *they* were concerned, but that wasn't the end of it. It meant that *I* was alone as well.

Even in that car, with my mother–the closest human being to my universe to ever exist–I was absolutely alone. I accept this now, as I've said, or at least I've come to somewhat of an understanding with it, but to a six-year-old boy it was a staggering revelation.

I tried to talk to my mother then, tried to explain the fear this concept had caused me–tried to get her to explain it away and make things better. Wasn't happening. First she smiled at me, told me I was being silly. Then, when I continued to pester her with it, when I couldn't let it go–she got angry. One car, two worlds. It felt as if the carpet had been yanked out from beneath my universe.

I was scared witless, frightened as I'd never been before. In the face of this, after hearing what had frightened me in my own words --or my explanation of those words as interpreted through the lens of my mother's world–she felt amusement, then anger, but no fear ... no understanding.

A friend of mine once recounted a similar experience. He was an artist, or could have been, if he'd stuck with it. He could draw like you wouldn't believe, and he could make the things he drew seem real. He was also obsessed, had been since *he* was a child.

He'd been drawing along, pretty as you please, forming vases and walls and doorways, learning the magic of perspective, when it hit him. There were no lines in or around the things he was drawing. On the paper, everything was separated from everything else by the dark borders of his pencil outlines. There were borders. There were limits. On the real wall, or around the real vase of flowers he'd been drawing, there were none.

"How can I draw," he wondered, "if there are no lines? If there are no lines, what keeps me from being part of that vase? What makes me different from the floor or the pencil in my hand?"

Of course, his mother laughed. Of course, she next got angry–very similar world to my own mother, I'd say, though I'd of course be wrong. None of them are the same.

So there he was–by the time I met him, 21 years old–still trying to figure out how to draw without using any lines. He also still had the anxiety attacks that came with the knowledge that if there were no lines, there was nothing keeping things out of one another. I tried to explain to him that all of those things he wasn't separate from were in his own world anyway, and that as long as they were part of *his* world and not someone else's, it was nothing to worry about. Of course, he didn't understand. He never will, not the same way that I do.

There are certain moments that I remember more clearly than others. I read a lot–mostly about people who seem the most cut off. Serial killers are all like that. Sociopaths, they call them. I call them realists. They understand that nothing beyond their own world matters. They understand that no matter how safe a society might seem, it only takes a small slip from the "norm" before they begin to hound and persecute you out of their own insecurity. A part of them knows the society is bullshit, but they mostly have that part locked away pretty deep inside. To look at them, you'd think they really *did* see the same things.

I read a book recently by a man named Straub, writing as a man named Underhill, writing about characters that may or may not have existed in the lives of one or the other of them. Worlds within worlds. In it, he mentions a photograph, front page of the New York Times the day after Ted Bundy was fried. I was obsessed, so I went and looked it up, and there it was. Louise Bundy, communicating for the last time with her son before his execution, their last connection immortalized.

That photograph is a perfect illustration of my concept. She was calling him from her own little world, of course, and in that world she believed that none of the places where her son's world and that of society had meshed were real. She believed that she could turn back the hands of the clock to the time when he was her "good boy."

He was never that person. That person was a figment of her own imagination, a construct that took the place in her own world inhabited by the world that was her true son. I wondered if he'd seen the houses along the road, as I had, or if he'd tried to draw the vases without lines. Maybe he just saw doorways into other people's worlds, and he went through them at will. He certainly seemed to be able to gain their trust. I think that Ted found a way out, if only for a little while, a way into other worlds. I think John Wayne Gacy found one too.

My own world becomes stagnant, at times. It would be refreshing to enter another, to understand how someone else understands, if you get my meaning.

Even if Louise Bundy could have maintained complete contact with her son throughout the execution, she would never have seen his world. No telling what might have happened in hers, though. Maybe old Teddy would've come waltzing in for the first time, face to face with his creator—maybe he'd even have said "Heeere's Johnny!" I'd kind of like to know for sure, but then, my impressions would never be quite the same as his, or hers, would they?

That same book I read, by Straub/Underhill/whoever, held another insight for me. All of the introspective writers have that quality. They make you think. Maybe things could be different. In Vietnam, says Underhill, he met a man named Dengler. The world they walked through over there, endless jungles, short little men who looked different and didn't operate in the "American" mode of "society," ate away at them. The "world," their term for reality back here at home, faded slowly into the background. The Earth itself made noises. Dengler said, "I think that's what happens when you're out here long enough. The edges melt." Maybe he should have met my friend—he could have found out that it's okay if they melt, there are no edges—no lines, either.

The lines melt too. When you separate yourself long enough, concentrating on the only world that matters, your own, the lines on the vases disappear, the relationship of time to reality becomes less important, and the barriers melt away. Your world, in my world, is different. Your world in my world is mine. This is the fundamental truth that I have discovered in over thirty years of research, the fundamental truth that I can't even explain to you, but that is no less true. In my world, I am God. In my version of your world, I am God, still. John knew.

In John Wayne Gacy's world, the tiny universe of a man named after a big, slow-talking actor who drank too much and didn't like black people, John Wayne Gacy, was God. He even constructed his own hell, beneath the floor of his home. That is one of the things that make me believe that he knew. I wonder if he stole the clown thing from Stephen King?

I read a lot, sorry to digress. I just wonder–when the bodies were pulled from beneath his house, bloated and rotting–did they hear a sinister, Tim Curryesque voice floating up through the drain?

"Down here, we bloat ... we all bloat."

Writers fascinate me. Within their own worlds, they create others, worlds within worlds, and they share them. We can't do that with our true worlds. When someone kills thirty-three people and gets caught, they fry him and celebrate. When someone creates a serial killer in his mind, imagines that killer's life and thoughts as his own, if only for a short time, and puts it on paper, he is paid the big bucks and labeled as a genius. A creative talent.

Maybe it's just a payoff. Maybe they read about killers that can't hurt them, and they thank the writer for capturing the "evil" on the paper and not releasing it into "society." Maybe they just envy the writer his release. Or maybe they have just a hint of the desire that I have; the desire to find a way into other worlds.

One question about these writers remains, for me: do the edges melt when they write? Are they fully in their own world at the moment of creation? Maybe they create a new world that they can slip into at will, enjoying freedoms there that they are denied by the concept of society? Do the characters have lines, or do they blend one to another? Is each character in his or her own little world? Gods in a pantheon? Good questions.

I tried writing myself. Thought I'd push the boundaries a little, see what came of a little creative hack and slash on the old keyboard. Nothing came of it. Either there is no magic there of the type I sought, or I just don't have the talent to bring it forth. Not that my plots were lacking. It was just that, whenever some creation of mine began to put his fingers around a young woman's throat, or to bash a particularly innocent young man's face against a wall, I didn't want my fingers on the keys. I wanted my fingers wrapped in soft skin, or banded like steel across a pliant throat.

Description falls short of reality every time, and the visions in my head only screamed the louder for release as my fingers and mind failed to bind them to paper. The lines did not melt, they solidified. My characters were trapped within them, and even I could not set them free. I couldn't reach them at all. I was still stuck in my own little world, no help for it there.

For every question, I am told, there is an answer. I would modify that to say that for every question there are as many answers as there are people, or worlds, but it is sufficient to know that there *is* an answer for me. The question? How can I get into another man's world–how can I become his God? It is possible that this is only happens at the moment of death, but somehow I believe there is another way. I am going to find out today–tonight.

I've been working off that death angle for several years, and while it is satisfying in its own way, it is incomplete. I can become another man's God by destroying his world forever. This I know. I have seen it in their eyes, felt it seeping from wounds and rattling through throats on the heels of proverbial last breaths. In that moment, that final moment where they look into my eyes and truly *see* me, our worlds collide. That is also the shortcoming of death–it is only a final *moment*. I want more than that.

That is why I stood there, watching and waiting, moving with the crowd as it lived and breathed a separate life of its own, a temporary bonding of all those souls who just couldn't keep away. It is a life-form more closely aligned with Gacy's own world than they might believe. They have all come here expecting–praying, even–for one thing. They want a man to die. They want to be the pantheon that rules his world. They want it as a memory to put on the self in their own worlds.

Granted, he was a dangerous man by any standards, particularly those of "society," but a man nonetheless. A man with vision beyond their own. Watching the hungry looks on their faces as they waited, I was reminded of the gladiators in Rome.

There's a visual for you. Gacy and Dahmer at forty paces, silverware to the death–battle until the second course is served. It might help pay for all those people languishing in the prison system, their own worlds shrinking in around them until they take up no more air or energy than a parking space. It might also prove another interesting study into the way those who gather to watch executions react to violent entertainment.

In two hours, give or take a minute or two, John Wayne Gacy will cease to exist. I will not. His world will be vacant, or what his world represents in my own, and I will step in. I have essentially already done so. That simple. Gacy is out, I am in. The sequel.

It's taken a lot of planning, but, hey, what have I got but time? The house wasn't so tough. His plans were on file with the city, just like any others, and the diagrams in the magazine spreads and the paper made recreation of the "hell" beneath it all a snap. Maybe, since Hell is in place already, I'll put a little effort into heaven–for the truly good ones, of course. It's a thought.

Stagnancy is not the goal. I believe he was on the right track, making progress, and I plan to pick up where he left off. It will be my interpretation of his world, of course, but I've been pretty thorough, and I believe it will be close enough. I think I can work myself in before everything snaps shut, before his world is banished to the ether. His world, my insight–the sky is the limit.

I find that the folks in the Jaycees are a friendly bunch. They took me right in, especially when they saw how many hours of volunteer service they could wring out of me. Upstanding citizen. Fund raiser. Not a family man, yet, or a father, but I have all the time in the world–John's world. He won't be using it. I thought about sending him a thank you note, but why ruin his last few hours? Let him die the God he was in life–if I'm right, he'll know soon enough–he'll be with me, and he'll be out of life.

The crowd is surging forward now, near the end, but I've hung back. Nothing to see from the outside, anyway, and I have other things to do, other worries. I've been careful with the paint, base-coat of white, big red balls for cheeks and three colors of blue lining the outside of my eyes in stars (always wanted them to say I had stars in my eyes). My face is even registered–painted on an egg-shell and registered as mine, and mine alone. They do that for you when you graduate clown school. Not an easy thing to do, in reality. There's more to the world of a clown than most people realize. Certainly more than

I realized. Everyone might love a clown, but they don't necessarily love themselves. Not all the frowns on clowns are painted on, believe me. More of those masks are really hiding something than not. Another revelation.

Another insight as well. A new face, a new world? Construction worker face–society world. Clown face, surreal world. John's *real* face? Only dead men can explain that one to you, dead men, and maybe John himself, and he's still claiming innocence.

Some of the people brought their children to the execution. Pretty tacky, I say, but what the heck? What's the lesson here, it's bad to kill? It's fun to watch people die? Beware the Boogey Man? I don't really care what their motives were in making it a family affair; It gives me a chance to practice. Maybe you saw me on the news the day after. I was carrying a sign–there were other clowns there besides myself, we all had signs. Mine was painted bright orange and red. Clown colors. "Clowns Make People Laugh, John," mine says. Nobody is laughing at John. The children smile when they look my way, but nobody is really laughing at me today, either. That's fine.

My little hell is waiting at home, and there is plenty of time. They will see me, and they will laugh. When I wear the clown face, live in the clown world, they will find me funny as hell. Others will come to me, and they will work with me at the little construction firm I've started–only a sub-contracting business, so far, but with plans for expansion. They will trust me, and they will drink with me in my construction worker world, and when I put on the paint and prance for their children, they will laugh at me too.

In the end, I will steal their worlds. I will be their God. It will be simple–everybody loves a clown.

The Fishmonger

The fishmonger screeched
From the corner of fourth and vine,
Flinging his hands out
Like a prophet, fish oil droplets
Glistening– flung diamonds,
Ripe with the stench of the depths,
The scales, not to be forgotten,
Clung to his yellowed nails…
And no one came to buy
As the rickety rust-caked Ferris wheel
Creaked in circles, I-beam serpents
Eating their own tails,
And a battered jukebox cranked
The one tune it remembered,
Spitting "Champagne Supernova to the sky"

Redemption

The Reverend Bookheim stood silently in the shadows beneath a large, neon sign that proclaimed "Live Sex Shows Nightly" in glowing pink letters. As the light strobed on and off, his shadow leaped to full length on the pavement, then receded to the blackness that had spawned it.

She was beautiful. Her slender legs were bare beneath a short, skin-tight skirt. Her long hair was pulled up in a ponytail that hung loosely over one shoulder and dangled between budding breasts. Sixteen, seventeen tops. Her makeup was heavy, but on her it was exotic rather than gaudy. There was something in those features, something haunting that called out to him ... something familiar.

He stepped into the dim light of the street and started toward her, pulling the brim of his hat down to shield his eyes and adjusting his dark sunglasses nervously. No one would know him here, no one that mattered. There were women–several of them–women who knew him only too well, but would never admit it. This wasn't a place he could expect to run into members of his congregation.

Back in Lavender, California, his face was well known. His church, "The Church of New Light," was the largest evangelical body in the area, and his radio show was broadcast up and down the length of the west coast. Here he was a shadow, a hungry shadow, aching for things that only the street, and the nameless faces he'd met there, could give him.

She spotted him immediately, and he noted with a quick thrill of pleasure the subtle shift in her stance. She placed a hand on her hip and let it ride there for a second before sliding it down to smooth the skirt across her thigh in a slow, sensual motion. Her eyes locked onto his and never looked away, and her lips were parted slightly, inviting. She was perfect.

As he came abreast of her, she called out in a voice that was barely more than a whisper. "You want a date, Mr.?"

He stopped, pretending to hesitate, as though eager to move on.

"What did you have in mind?" he asked, his throat dry. She was even more enticing up close and he saw her gaze drop to his crotch, then return to meet his own, a smile planted firmly on her deep, red lips. Her eyes were alight with the energy of youth, but there was a wisdom in those depths, as well–a strength that nearly made him turn and walk away. There was a hunger there to match his own.

"Let's say I'm a bad girl," she purred, moving closer, so close that her nipples brushed the front of his jacket and the scent of her perfume wafted up to confuse his thoughts. "I need someone to ... punish me."

Bookheim closed his eyes and reached deep for control. Too much. It was too much, too soon, and they were still on the street, vulnerable. Why did these damnable little whores insist on meeting on the street? It was like a long, drawn-out, sinful dance, and even after years on the dance floor, he could be manipulated here as easily as a schoolboy.

"How much," he grated.

"You a cop?" she countered quickly, sliding an arm around his back and turning him so that they were walking together down the street.

"No," he said gruffly, shaking his head, "of course not."

"I've got to ask, you know," she said, letting the tip of her tongue brush his earlobe as she whispered into his ear. "One hundred, seventy-five for me, twenty-five for the room."

He nodded. It was high, more than he'd ever spent, but he had to have her, and she knew it. The trembling in his shoulders must have given him away. He had no patience, or time, for bickering. She was bad, alright, evil incarnate, and he needed her like he'd never needed anyone, or anything in his life.

They rounded a corner, and another neon sign came into view–The Shady Cove Inn. The "o" in cove was burned out, and the braces that held the entire sign sagged away from the wall, giving way slowly to the drag of gravity. Bookheim imagined the weight of all the sins that had been committed behind those walls weighing down on it, burying it, pressing it toward its inevitable place in the kingdom below. He imagined his own sins at the top of that pile…his breath quickened, and he pulled her ahead more quickly.

She didn't protest. She had melted to his side the moment he'd nodded at her price, her motions coordinating themselves with his, their steps synchronized, their flesh molded together at every possible angle that did not prevent forward motion. He felt like a moth, or a fly, trapped in the silken web of a beautiful, but dangerous spider.

They slipped through the door of the Shady Cove Inn quietly and into the dusty, smoke-drenched interior. As they passed beneath it, Bookheim flinched away from the blinking sign. He felt its weight on his shoulders, felt the weight of the sin on his soul. Brushing it aside, he stepped into another world.

They passed through a nearly deserted lobby. The furniture had faded to unknown colors with dust so deeply imbedded in the cushions that it rose to hover in small wisping clouds above the cushions like smoke.

One old man sat in the corner, dealing cards into a solitaire layout. His eyes were fixed on the smoke-crusted front window. His hands moved mechanically, the only sound the soft whisk of the cards sliding over one another, that and the creaking of the chair in the other corner of the lobby.

As the girl released him momentarily to lean forward over the check-in desk, he turned toward that sound. There was a woman seated in the chair, her eyes glassy, staring at and through him at once. There was a thin string of drool extending from her top lip down to her chin. Her lips were moving, mumbling, and endless cascade of words he could not hear–did not want to hear. There was something about her that he knew, something he recognized.

She rocked back and forth slowly, like a macabre metronome. He felt drawn to her, hypnotized. His mind spun through dark fantasies–was she a demon? Was the dark one come to haunt him, mocking him with open acknowledgment of his sin? He strained, trying to make out what she was saying, trying to be certain that there was no light of recognition in her vacant eyes, no accusation in the twitching of her lip.

"Hey," a soft voice whispered in his ear. She was back, as closely knit to his form as if she'd grown there, as natural–and evil–as ever. "You see something you like better, or are you ready to go?"

Bookheim ripped his gaze from the old woman's form and turned to her, anger flashing in his eyes, dying in the cool wash of her beauty. She caught the flash, but she was not afraid. She drew him in, drew him along, and before he knew what was happening they were moving past the clerk and up the dingy stairs to the next level.

As they passed the counter, he averted his eyes, slouched a bit and moved furtively. He hated this moment, the moment of control granted to the owners and managers of these cheap little dives over those who frequented them. He could be exposed, he could be refused. He could be ridiculed, made sport of by a man who, though he had little money, no future, and a dead-end job, was in control of his life for a few precious moments. He didn't pay for his fantasies, didn't hide away from those who might recognize his face. He belonged here, it was Bookheim that was the outcast.

The stairs creaked beneath their feet, and dust rose from the aging wood, making him sneeze. Somehow it didn't matter. Her perfume mingled with that dust, transformed it, and it became part of the experience. Where her skin brushed his it burned like fire.

Hellfire a voice whispered in his head.

Where her breath dampened his skin, her tongue tickled at his earlobe, was the chill of ice. It shivered through him, crashing against the walls of heat she'd created and shattering his resolve. She knew what he wanted, damn her, and she wasn't going to give him even a chance to tell her.

They stopped before one of the identical, faceless doors, each opening to its own world of depravity and darkness. The empty hall was a gateway. He knew this, and all those others who found what they needed in such places knew it as well. There was the real world, his congregation, his faith, and there was this world–the dream world. The world where a little money could bring him the things he'd never been able to find for himself, where happiness, in small bursts, could be bought and paid for–where flesh was a commodity amd sin was the law.

She slipped the key into the lock and it turned silently. The door opened and they entered, never separating. The door closed behind them with a soft snick, leaving them in darkness, and she turned him to face her, pressed herself into his body and drew him down so their tongues could meet.

He ran his hands down the length of her dark hair, felt the shudders begin deep within him and burst toward the surface. Felt her swallowing him whole.

"Come," she whispered, drawing him across the room. As his eyes accustomed themselves to the dim light, he saw that there was little furniture in the room, a dresser, which was cloaked in shadows, a sagging bed, and a small table with withered flowers in its center. Two chairs.

They moved to the bed, and she seated him gently on the edge of it, pulling free of his embrace. He felt the mattress drop lower under his weight, felt the press of rusted springs from within. The whining creak of protest from the frame echoed in the silence, hanging in the air like a last accusation—a cry to his soul. He shivered and sweat coated every inch of his body. He didn't reach up to brush it from his eyes, but allowed the stinging, saltiness of it to blur his vision, blinding him to his surroundings, creating of her a soft, curved silhouette of desire...his desire. It was not about her, after all—he'd paid her to enter his little world, to *become* his little world.

She moved before him, slowly. There was no music, but he could almost hear the notes behind her motion, could almost feel the rhythm, the pulsing backbeat that moved her, invading his mind. As she swirled and gyrated, her scent rose with the dust, swirling about him and robbing him of a bit more reality. She was dragging him down. He imagined that he could hear the devil laughing, calling out to him, and welcoming him. He shook his head and concentrated on her, only her. The guilt, the repentance, they could come later.

Her clothing disappeared piece by piece, drawn seductively over smooth skin and tossed aside, fluttering to the dusty floor, revealing more and more as she continued to sway and grind. Her eyes were locked on his, the intensity of her gaze defining his emotions. For a moment he considered leaving, jumping up and running until his legs would no longer sustain the effort. None of the others had been like this.

They had been dead inside–hollow. On the outside smiles, condescending endearments–playing a part. They had been adequate easy to distance himself from afterward. This was different. She was teasing him into her game, urging him to levels he'd only dreamed about ... levels he'd never dared to attempt with any of the hollow women. Levels of depravity for which he feared there might be no redemption. She wanted his soul, and he was granting her wish–willingly.

"Who are you?" He breathed, trying to rise, falling back weakly–captivated.

She moved a few inches closer, so that her eyes were clearly visible through the smoky, dusty air.

"I am whoever you want me to be," she purred. "I am whoever you need me to be."

Though she offered him control with her words, he knew it was a false promise. As she slid over him, her naked flesh pressing into his clothing, her fingers working at his belt, lowering his zipper, he knew he was hers. He was paying her to take him, and the thought thrilled him. All of the others he had ruled, he had owned for a short time, rented from the street. This one would take him, and he found he had no strength to resist her.

"Who are you?" he asked again.

She didn't speak. She smiled at him, pulling his shirt aside and off over his shoulders, dropping her lips to his flesh and nibbling with small, white teeth. Her hair floated over him like the silk of his vestments, and he drank in the scent of her, strained up to meet her roving lips, to offer himself, to not let the contact be broken.

She pressed him down again. Seemingly from nowhere she'd brought forth a silken scarf from beside him.

"Do you trust me?" she asked, lowering her eyes shyly.

"Why?" he replied.

"I want to show you something, to give you something, but you have to trust me. You have to let me do what I want."

"Anything," he said, realizing how helpless he sounded and reveling in it, "anything, just … don't stop."

She nodded almost imperceptibly, then reached for his wrist and looped the scarf around it, pulling it quickly into a slipknot. Before he could protest she'd brought forth another, and it was sliding around his free arm—pulling tight. He realized that she'd been prepared for this. The scarves were already looped around the legs at the head of the bed.

"I …" he didn't know what to say. He'd been ready to protest, but what would he protest? Her hands were massaging his flesh again, moving down to slide his pants toward his knees, and he moved to assist in any way he could, wriggling from the now offensive clothing, pressing toward her groping fingers and praying she would remove his underpants. He couldn't think beyond that, so he focused on it. She could leave him as he was, and the helplessness of that combined with the guilt, the obsessive need for flesh that had driven him to this seedy room, this surreal world of sin and darkness in the first place, to drive him mad with frustration.

Then her fingers slid around the elastic band, and he felt the last remaining barrier between them falling away. He lay back against the musty sheets in sudden relief. He almost didn't notice when another scarf captured his left ankle, and a fourth his right. He was beyond protest…she had to finish what she'd started. She had to relieve the pressure she'd brought to him. If she wanted more money, it was hers–all of it–more than he'd brought, more than he'd ever dreamed he might pay. Anything.

"Don't stop," he pleaded.

"I won't," she breathed, suddenly beside him again, he hands working his flesh, sliding through the twisting hairs on his chest, moving slowly down to cup him. As she slid over him once more, her silken flesh now pressed to his own, the sweat of his passion mingling with the scent of her perfume, she began to speak again, softly and slowly, so quietly and quickly that he could scarcely make out the words. Each time he nearly had it–each time comprehension threatened to invade his mind, she would emphasize a word with a stroke of her hand, or punctuate a statement with the tip of her tongue, seeking his, moving away, exploring every inch of him as if she were starving for him–withering without his touch.

"I want to help you," she said. "I want to bring you home. I am the way. I want to give you something special, something you need."

The words were like a litany, a prayer. She slid over him, encasing him within her, and he was surprised–shocked by the warmth of her, the moist heat. She panted, and he saw that her dark hair was matted to her face, her eyes closed and her tongue constantly moving, wetting her lips, uttering small sounds that intertwined with the words she continued to speak. If he'd believed in witchcraft, he'd have thought it a spell, and he the victim, because it would not have mattered at that moment if she'd been informing him she was collecting his soul for hell, he could not have done a thing about it, and *would* not have, if he could.

The hollow women had never been like this. Nothing of themselves had been a part of the bargain. They rented their flesh, a few of the better ones offered a meager acting talent, but the fantasy world was his alone. They allowed him to drag their bodies into his little world, but whatever might remain, deep inside their skewed thoughts, was off limits. This was different.

The passion of her motions, the urgency of the constant flow of her words, rising and falling in time with urgent breaths and slow, sinuous gyrations of hip and thigh, all of it drew him in deeper. Hers was a world of heat, and she shared it eagerly, wantonly. Fanatically. The monotonous chanting of her voice drowned out the sounds of the street, cut off the sights and scents of the room surrounding them. He could make out little of what she said, and yet each intonation, each coherent syllable, wove her net tighter.

"Only through me," she whispered. "Only through me, mother ... home."

Everything blurred into an insanity of heat and release. The sweat rolled down his face, into his eyes, turning her swaying form into a surreal silhouette, a fuzzy-edged angel surrounded by a glowing halo of light that burned like fire. Her words brought him to a level of need beyond thought, shared that moment with him–*desired* it. She pulled his seed from him, drew it within her and shuddered as the touch of it released her own climax, drove her up, down, whirled her wildly about as she clung to him with digging nails and clenching knees.

Pain blended to light, and back to pain. His body arched–released, trapped at that moment of ultimate pleasure for an eternity wherein they were one–indiscernible–joined body and soul. Released. He nearly blacked out from the snap-back to reality, draining into her in ever-weakening bursts of helpless sacrifice.

She did not withdraw, sliding downward instead, clutching at him with muscles he wouldn't have dreamed to exist, clinging to him as if fearing she might miss some drop of him, some vital link she was unwilling to relinquish.

Now she was silent, and the void created by that silence was deafening. He turned his gaze up to hers, feeling as if for the first time the bite of the silk on his wrists, the restraining tug of the bonds on his ankles. She didn't meet his gaze at first, and he made a small, whimpering sound. She didn't have to acknowledge him, and he feared, deep in his heart, that she would just leave him. No words, no solace, no release.

She turned to him, though, and her smile was exalted–her features radiant. Where they'd seemed cheap and exotic they were glowing with released emotion, with triumphant abandon.

"Who are you?" he asked again. "Who ..."

She shook her head quickly. She took one long, nailed finger and touched him on the throat, traced a line straight down the center of his chest–lingering to feel the trip-hammer rhythm of his heart–continuing downward to the point where she straddled him, weaving it up and through her glistening pubic hairs, then back down and up until it came to rest on his lips. He wanted to speak, to protest, but he felt the stirring of new desire in his cooling flesh, felt himself rise against her–saw her smile.

She slid over and off of him and dropped to her knees on the soiled carpet. She clasped her hands before her and laid them softly across his chest. She laid her head down, her forehead on her thumbs, her hair cascading out and over him, tickling at his nose and chin, caressing the length of the erection that he could not control–that threatened, once again, to control him.

He couldn't reach up to brush her hair away, and it maddened him. He turned his face to one side, then to the other, but all the motion served to do was to fuel the flames that were washing through him. He was trembling, shaking with need, and he felt–with shame–the arch of his back, the wanton press of his flesh against her supine form.

He heard her speaking softly again, felt the moist touch of her lips coating his skin with a soft dampness, evaporating, returning with each breath. The desire was growing in strength, threatening to envelop him completely, and he allowed another sound to pass his lips–a plea–a low moan of such desire that he felt her hesitate, felt her head rise from her hands.

She rose, stood beside him and gazed into his eyes. Her own were distant, the smile playing over her trembling lips unnerving. She let one hand fall to his cheek, turned him to face her more completely–searching for something in his eyes and apparently finding it.

"I must leave you," she said softly.

"No!" His outburst was sudden, jarring–out of place in the dark, wet aftermath of their lovemaking.

She placed her finger over his lips again, and he could taste her, could feel the scent of their joining seeping into him, altering the world around them again, skewing his thoughts from their intended goal.

"I said I wanted to give you something, to help you," she reprimanded him gently. "You have to trust me."

Before he could protest, before the tumbling words could find his tongue, she was gone. The door snicked shut behind her with a finality that jarred the passion from his mind. He felt himself soften, dangling damp and useless against the musty sheets. The depravity of the moment began to seep into his consciousness. The enormity of his situation began to play at the edges of his understanding.

He heard the sounds of reality returning in her wake. Outside the dusty window he heard the hiss of tires passing on the streets below. He heard the voices of the hollow women, calling out to passersby. He heard the honking of horns and the quick pounding of guilty feet. He heard the snapping, crackling buzz of the drooping neon sign–so close to the window that the sign's illumination painted the dingy walls of the darkened room a deep, dripping red. It reminded him of stained glass, of the altar at the church. The voices from without became the buzz of the congregation.

He couldn't cry out. He could not be found like this. She had said he must trust her, and yet she had long since removed the possibility of any other action on his part. She would come, or she would not. If he were found by any other, if she disappeared into the darkness of the streets and he never saw her again, his life would be over. His career. His faith.

He knew she had robbed him. He knew the soul of the hollow women, knew their emptiness–their helplessness. His destiny had been stripped from him; his soul had willingly drained itself into her eager, needy flesh. The desperate depth of his sin seemed to roll from him in beads of sweat, joining with the compounded sins that the room had collected–that the sheets beneath him had known. In passionate shame, he needed her.

He lay in silence, and after a while he prayed–his words beginning slowly, and then speeding until they became incoherent, meaningless. He spoke to a void, to the emptiness of the room. Tears stung his eyes, blurring the room again, this time to private hell of punishment and despair. Sweat dripped across his flesh, and he could not wipe it away. It burned in the furrows left by her nails, eating its way into him, making him one with the sin and burning it into him with pain and fire.

There was no way to know for sure how long he lay like that, how long it took for darkness to rise and claim him. He had strained at his bonds until the soft silk ripped at him like cutting wire. He had fought the itching, sticky sensations, like the feet of tiny insects transiting the length of his flesh, until the urge to scream had nearly overcome his control. Darkness was not a relief. It swallowed him into a nightmare world from which only her wild eyes and chanting voice might draw him back.

He awakened to odd, flickering light. She was at his side, and as he swept his head from side to side, he saw that every horizontal space in the room was covered in candles–red candles. Their flames leaped and danced, sending crazy shadows to race up and down the walls as she gazed down at him adoringly.

When she saw his eyes flicker open, she moved to him instantly, pressing her naked flesh to his tightly. He felt soiled, dirty, and he realized that the pain he felt was a furious need to urinate.

"Please," he said weakly, "I have to get up … you have to untie me."

She shook her head again. When she saw him glance down at his penis, saw the swollen mass of it, she leaned down and retrieved something from beneath the bed. It was a pitcher–an insulated coffee pitcher.

"Let me help," she said, grabbing his testicles in one hand and slipping the cold plastic mouth of the pitcher over him.

He fought miserably for control, lost. He watched her smile again as he released in a rush. She held him gently until he finished, pulled the pitcher away and carried it almost reverently into the small bathroom–more like a broom closet with a commode and a small, dingy sink. He watched the doorway intently every second she was away, watched her return with a damp cloth in her hand.

She let it fall to his thigh, and then began to wash him slowly and carefully, not turning to meet his eyes.

"You have to let me go," he said softly. "I have to …"

She moved the cloth slowly up and down the length of his penis, and to his dismay, it rose once more to her ministrations. He closed his eyes, thought of the old women in the front pews at Sunday worship, thought of the toilets at the county fair, thought of his father's cold, arrogant face as he'd brought the belt up and back, up and back. Nothing could wipe her from his mind. It was *her* mind now … his prison.

He grew in her hands and she leaned forward to kiss her handiwork, then turned to him finally.

"I've brought you something," she smiled. "I want to help you."

She slid over him again, lying atop him so that her eyes were so near to his that he saw the light of the candle flames dancing across their surface. She straddled him, lowered her head and clasped her hands on his chest. It was a position of supplication, of prayer.

He felt himself rise against her. She was speaking again, softly as before, and without missing a beat she lifted her hips and positioned herself so that he slipped within her. He moaned, but she settled over him, not moving, holding him tightly.

There was another sound. He hadn't noticed it before, but now the girl's words seemed to bring it forth–a creaking, squealing noise. There were words, as well, words that did not come from her mouth, but from the direction of the other sound.

He craned his neck to the side, forcing himself to look, forcing his eyes to penetrate the glare of the candles on the dresser. He saw a dark shape, cloaked in shadows, moving back and forth, up and back.

"Who is that?" he asked fearfully, trying vainly to struggle against her.

The girl ignored him, continuing as she had. When he fought harder, trying to roll her to one side, or to pull himself free, she rode his struggles, matching the rhythmic movement of the shadow in the corner, rocking to the creaking, squealing beat.

She raised her head then, and he saw her eyes. Memory snapped into focus, supplanting reality, and it was not this girl that rode him, but another. There had been nothing wild about that other girl, nothing exciting, other than that she'd been willing to sacrifice herself to him.

He remembered. She had been so young, so simple. He'd had her, then, when she'd turned up pregnant, threatening his burgeoning career as a man of God, he'd sent her away.

"You must leave," he'd said, righteous anger powering his voice. "Your sin drags us both down, and you must find redemption." They had been empty words. He'd wanted her gone.

He'd given her money. There was a clinic in a small town upstate, a town where she claimed to have relatives. He'd never seen her again. Until now. But this was not her. This could never be her.

The girl's gaze was still locked to his, and she smiled down at him. "I've planned for this moment," she said softly, undulating her hips. "I've learned–studied what would please you–become what you need. You are empty, but I can fill you– I can bring you home."

His flesh betrayed him to her, even as he shook his head in negation. The figure in the corner was moving now, rising from the chair and hobbling toward them. He saw the long, straggly hair and the rheumy, yellowed eyes. Her smile was wide, and despite the drool that still lingered on her chin, her expression was animated. Words–prayers–spun from her lips like webs, dropping over the girl, over him, binding them even more tightly.

He felt withered, cold hands on his thigh, caressing his chest; the scent of urine and old sweat invaded his senses. Still he moved against the softness of the girl's body. The heat enveloped him, the candle-light danced and the old woman swayed like a pendulum at his side.

The girl leaned closer once more, clamped down on him and drew him within her so fully that he feared immersion–feared he would never pull free.

"Who … are … you?" he gasped, dreading the answer, praying he was wrong --- needing her not to stop.

"I told you I would give you something," she whispered, sliding over him like a wave of molten heat until their lips were only a hair's breadth apart, until their breath was a single taste– their hearts a synchronous beat. "Something mother was never able to do. I want to make you happy. I've studied, you know," she paused to run her tongue in and out of his ear, up the side of his cheek, down to meet his own. He involuntarily met her advance–drank deeply from her lips.

"I've dedicated my life to this moment," she whispered, "and Mother has prayed. She does nothing else now; the prayer is her life–our life."

She rose above him, enveloping him once more in the heat of her presence, dragging his sanity from him in pulsing bursts.

"Won't you pray with us, Father?"

Revelation

The seventeenth configuration
Of stars,
     In conjunction with the proper illumination
Of neon signs on cafes, and bars,
Birthed an epic transformation, An arcane celebration,
A revelation that encroached on the darkness
Claimed dominion.
Souls set free, spirits unbound,
     And everything on sale, one night only,
Sitting back on his heels and smiling,
God whispered.
"That is so COOL"

Swarm

Morado woke to pain. It surrounded him, filled his thoughts, and yanked with dark glee at the endings of the nerves in his leg and the right side of his face. He couldn't focus on his surroundings, couldn't make out any distinct sound over the roaring in his ears. It took what seemed hours to realize that the roaring was the beating of his heart, the rushing sound the harsh intake and expulsion of his breath.

As control returned to his mind, the pain localized, sending sharp, searing bolts through his right leg. His face was numb–his right cheek pressed into the soft, moist earth–and when he lifted his head he gave a hoarse shout of horror. Bits and pieces of his skin had remained behind. It had adhered to the ground, a mass of buzzing insects and seared flesh. He could still see–his eyes were intact, but when he brought his hand up to what had been his right cheek, he couldn't bring himself to touch it. He didn't want to know. It was bad, that was enough to know. Any more would eat away at his sanity, and as the reality of his situation began to coalesce in his mind, he realized he would need every iota of that sanity in the hours to come.

Probably, it would not be enough.

He wasn't certain where he was. That fact clicked into place in the forefront of his mind, and he felt the sweat drip down his forehead. He didn't know where the others were, either. They'd been moving inland, away from the base. Every nerve had been taut—every instinct on edge. This was no game. It was good money, but not easy. That was the way of the mercenary. All of the easy assignments fell to those with families and homes; all the suicide missions went to the hired help, to the trained guerrillas with combat experiences and death wishes.

They'd been moving inland from an amphib drop, twelve in all, plus two native scouts. The objective was a village with a name Morado couldn't remember, let alone pronounce. A suspected ammo dump. They'd traveled light, few supplies and fewer hopes of success, but as usual, the money offered had been impossible to refuse. So had the challenge.

Morado knew almost nothing about the others, nothing beyond their faces, or their names, Billy D, Jules, The Hollow Man, Gray, soldiers in the endless war. He knew what was important about them, and that was enough. The war was important. It didn't matter what name it wore, or what language the participants spoke; all that mattered was that it continue, that they remain useful. One thing they had in common, this small band of mercenaries, was that they didn't fit well into polite society—families, relationships, jobs. This was their life, such as it was, and they knew full well it would end up as their deaths as well. That was fine—it was what they wanted.

Morado decided, though, that he didn't want that just yet. Not here, not like this. He pressed his hands into the soft earth and tried to lever himself to his knees. Pain stabbed through his leg, blanking his mind in a white-hot flash and dropping him back, face-first in the dirt. His mind whirled and the agony of his attempted movement was like a thousand daggers plunged one after the other through his skin.

Christ, he grated, pressing his teeth tightly together and clenching his fists. The realization that both of his hands and arms seemed to be functioning normally gave him a ray of hope, even as the searing pain in his leg threatened to drive him into unconsciousness.

He opened his eyes once more, and he saw the butt of his M-16 a few feet away. He snaked his arm out slowly, keeping his lower body as immobile as possible. It was just beyond the reach of his groping fingers. With a deep breath, he steeled himself against the pain, and began to crawl. The first inch nearly did him in, but as his mind became aware of the limits of the pain, he was able to establish a boundary between himself and the blackness, to incorporate the pain into the focus of his movements.

Another inch. His fingers brushed the rough plastic of the rifle butt, and he rested for a long breath. Insects swarmed over his face, and though he had no feeling, he could see them, could sense them violating his ruined skin, and he moved again. He had to get to his feet.

He managed to grip the rifle firmly, and he dragged it slowly toward him, pulling it tightly against his right side. It was obvious that his leg was going to be of little use–he was going to have to prop himself up and find a way to move on. The longer he stayed–wherever he was–the more chance of being discovered. The natives would bayonet him in place until the insects finished him and hang the remains among the vines as a warning to others who followed. Rest was not an option.

He looked about himself quickly. Their scouts had been moving ahead of the main force, hacking a way through the underbrush with machetes, but there was no sign of any of this from where he lay. He was surrounded by low-hanging vines and ferns. The hollowed-out space where he'd landed–that was the only way he could explain his presence there–was hidden from the jungle on all sides. There was no sign that anyone other than himself had *ever* been there, let alone in the last few hours.

He worked up his courage, practicing the breathing exercises the "Hollow Man" had taught him, pushed the pain back into a small, dark recess at the back of his mind and willed himself to rise. The Hollow Man claimed to be into Zen ... claimed to be a warrior of the spirit. Morado didn't know from spirit, but he knew when something worked, and he'd never seem an expression of emotion on the Hollow Man's face, even when he'd seen the man take a bullet to the thigh.

He pressed the rifle into the ground, taking as much weight as possible off of his right leg and praying that his left was uninjured. He managed to get upright by a combination of pulling on the branches overhead and levering himself up with his rifle, then he stood very still, focusing his concentration on the torture that was to come.

His memories were clearing, and he let his mind drift back. He needed to remember what had happened if he was going to find a way to survive. The scouts had been gone for an exceptionally long time. He remembered that. He also remembered how they'd all begun to feel nervous, as if there was something hanging in the air above them, waiting to pounce. It could be that way, sometimes, a foreign country, jungles far from anywhere, and only a few distant partners, lost in their own little worlds, for company.

Then he remembered the explosion. He nearly staggered and fell as the images hit him full force. Mines. They'd walked directly into a field of mines, no warning, no word from the scouts, just death and fire. Morado had been near the rear, and the bodies of the others had taken the brunt of the explosive force. He'd had time to see the light, to hear the sound, before it lifted him from his feet.

The images grew surreal, faces flashed past him, cries of pain and curses filled his mind. The Earth skewed, the sky where the ground should be, then trees. He felt the moment again where his right leg had come in contact with the trunk of a tree, slammed around it, flipping him upward again, and then down … down into a pool of suffocating darkness.

Mines. Either the scouts had set them up, or they, too, were dead. There were no other ways it would wash. His whirling mind was faced with the realization that, for some odd, impossible reason, the men who'd brought them here might have purposely led them to their deaths. War was an unforgiving god. There was no time to worry over the variables, like why. No time for anything, really, except to move, and to move as rapidly as possible, and to hope that there was something or someplace ahead of him that would allow him to survive. If not, he hoped there was a suitable place to die.

The path hadn't been far away, and he found it only moments after he began his slow, painful journey through the jungle. He'd used his knife to cut a crutch from one of the surrounding trees, and though it bowed under his weight, it held. He was able to move. When he reached the trail, however, he stopped.

They weren't there. The hole left by the mine was where he'd expected it. There were shreds of clothing, bits of weapons and packs lying about, but there were no bodies. The others were simply gone. He searched the area as well as he could, fearing every moment that he'd hit a second mine and end his problems, or that whoever had set them up in the first place would return and take him away as well, but he found no indication of how the bodies had been moved. There were no breaks in the underbrush to indicate anything had been dragged through, and the path itself showed their trail up to the point of the explosion, but nothing more. There were no footprints continuing along the line they'd traveled, and there was no indication of retreat.

Gone.

As he stood, leaning on his makeshift crutch and trying to put it into focus, the humming, buzzing hoard of insects that had followed him from his little clearing took advantage of the moment to swarm over his face. The sensitivity in his skin was beginning to return, and he felt them as a moving itch, felt them bite and violate his flesh. He brushed his hand across them rapidly, fighting off a sudden wave of nausea, and made up his mind. He would move forward, continuing on the line of travel they'd begun. If any of the others were alive, they might be there, and if not, there was the village. If he could get in quickly enough, he might be able to find shelter of some sort. More likely, they would kill him on sight, but that was a better option than dying as bug food in the jungle.

He started forward, both hands gripping the half-assed crutch he'd cut, his M-16 slung over his left shoulder and banging against his leg as he moved. He made his way down the trail slowly, his breath labored and the sweat pouring down to sting on his wounded face and to blind his eyes.

His steps became a monotonous rhythm. The jungle on both sides of the trail blurred to walls of green, the maze of vines and underbrush that covered the path absorbed the full concentration of his mind. The scouts might have continued in this direction, or not, but they'd not cleared the trail. It would have been slow going, even with two healthy legs … as it was, it was unending torture, and Morado found himself retreating further and further from the reality of the moment.

He stopped suddenly. To one side of the trail, he saw a mound rising up from the jungle floor. It didn't look like a normal ground formation. There was little or no vegetation covering it, and the earth was smooth, as if it had been shaped by hand. It rose to the height of a man, then receded again as he made his way around it. His mind flashed on images of Indian burial mounds he'd seen as a child, but this was far from that land–another culture, another world. They did not bury their dead here at all. They burned them.

He knew that he shouldn't be worrying over a mound of dirt. He should be worrying about making it through this alive. Something itched at him, though, something old, and familiar, and even as he turned away and moved further down the path, he couldn't let it go.

He was weakening. He felt it in the shortness of his breath, in the nausea that swam through his system with each step. Another of the strange mounds rose to his right, and he headed toward it. He would have to rest. He thought he might have one of the stimulant capsules he'd brought still in his pack, if he could get to it, and if he could force it down his dried, parched throat. His canteen was gone–and in his delirium, he'd not thought to look for it before he'd returned to the trail. A mistake. He wouldn't be granted many of those in a situation like this.

The earth was softer on the mound than it had been on the trail, loose and obviously piled there recently. He fell back against it roughly and let his mind blank for a few seconds as he caught his breath. He shifted slightly, searching for a more comfortable position, and the motion sent the pain slamming through his leg once more. When he'd been up, concentrating on staying erect, he'd been able to block that pain. Now it came rushing back in to claim him, pushing aside his weak attempts at control contemptuously.

He felt himself slipping back into the blackness, and he let it happen. He had no strength left to fight it. He pressed into the softness of the dark, rich soil, and he left the jungles behind.

He was walking in a field near his Uncle's farm—he recognized it immediately. The air was warm, very warm, and there was almost no breeze at all. He'd been sent to visit his cousins that summer—his twelfth. They were an unruly, brutish lot, more at home with pickup trucks and cattle than anything else. His parents had deemed it a "growing experience." Morado—Gabe, as they called him, short for Gabriel—had called it hell.

They'd been on him from the moment he arrived, making fun of the way he talked, the way he walked and dressed. He'd had nothing to fall back on. He was in their world, and all he could do was play along and hope he survived. He knew that that particular vacation had marked the point where survival had become his creed. Not just because of his cousins, but because of everything that happened.

The field beneath his feet was of mown hay, and the stalks of the plants lay dry and matted against the earth like a woven blanket. In the distance, he could see the lazy curve of the river. That was his goal.

His cousins had assured him that, if he made his way to just the right bend in the stream, he'd find the spot where, on the far bank, the girls form the neighboring farm went to swim.

"They ain't spent a lot of money on swimsuits, if you get my meaning," Juanito had told him, leering. "You never seen nothin' like this in that city, Gabe."

It had been a dare, of course. Any reason he'd have come up with not to go and have a look would have branded him a sissy, or worse, and he'd have been beaten. This way he got away from them for a while, got out where he could think a little. If he got to see naked farm girls cavorting in a river, well, that was just icing on the cake.

But there was something odd about the air around him—something that hung just beyond his senses. At first he thought it was just the surreal shimmer of the heat rising from the ground, but as his mind focused on it, he realized it was a soft hum, a vibration. It seemed to come from everywhere at once. The sound was hypnotic, and as he continued toward the river, it ate its way into his thoughts, dispersing daydreams of the river, and of his cousins. There was something powerful in that sound—a hint of danger that he couldn't pinpoint.

The sound grew louder, and he stopped for a moment, searching the field for the source. Along one side was a line of trees, in front of him the river, behind and to the other side nothing but open land. He searched the air for some sort of jet, shielded his eyes from the sun to search the visible length of the river for boats, but he found nothing.

He shrugged and turned toward the river again, his steps quickened by the nervous fear that seeped up through his thoughts. He tried to dismiss it, but as he moved forward, the sounds grew louder once more, droning, beating against his senses.

He began to run just as the first stinger pierced his flesh.

They were everywhere, hundreds of them, maybe thousands, slender black bodies glistening in the bright sunlight, their wings a hazy blur. He ran, but they seemed unhindered by any amount of speed he could muster. They clung to his head, to his back and shoulders, stinging, injecting him with their poison, swarming before his face. He flailed his arms wildly, knocking them aside, fighting to keep them from his eyes.

His steps were slowing, but he was near the river, and he focused on it, fought for it and blanked everything from his mind but that blue, shimmering surface. The hornets were frenzied, covering him like a second skin as he ran, piercing him, again and again. It was a dark, mind-rending race, his weakening strength and failing will against their relentless assault. The goal line was the water, the only hope of salvation.

He screamed once, but as he felt a soft, silky body slip past his lips and the stinger pass through the soft flesh of his tongue, he clamped down, crushing the insect between his teeth and forcing himself to swallow. His tongue swelled immediately, and he had to force himself to breathe, had to fight to get the air through to his tortured lungs. Despite the pain, there were no more screams. He'd learned an early lesson in survival.

Then the ground gave way beneath him, and only as he smashed bodily into the water beneath him did he realize he'd reached the bank of the river and fallen from the edge into the swirling water below.

As he fell, he heard screams from another source, other voice, saw a quick flash of tanned skin and long, blonde hair Then there was nothing but the water, dark–dragging him down–soothing the burning of his skin and finalizing his loss of breath. He dove deeper, then deeper still. Darkness even thicker and more cloying than that of the river reached out to claim him, and he fell into its embrace.

He never felt the hands grip his shoulders, lift him, and force him to the surface. He never felt the sudden cough of air that spewed river water and mud across his chest, emptying his lungs so a rush of warm, fresh air could bring him to a semblance of life. He remembered only the shining, black bodies, the droning of wings, and the darkness.

He felt the ground beneath him before he heard the sound, and he was at first unaware of the moment when the dream ended and reality returned. The pain in his leg dragged him from the dream, and he fought desperately to sort out his thoughts and open his eyes. He heard a droning buzz, and the vibration of the ground did not depart with his memories. The insects had clotted the side of his face, and with a super-human effort, he lifted one arm and brushed at them, clearing them as best he could. There was no way he could get to his feet again.

The sound was deafening now, maddening. His attention fixed on it. Choppers. They were coming in; someone was coming in–he turned painfully to his chest and began to scramble up the mound of dirt. He had to get up higher, up to where they could see him, where they would find him.

He couldn't get a view beyond the overhanging trees, so he concentrated on the ground. Nothing he could do to help by looking up, either they would see him, or he would die, but all he could do to help them along was to keep moving. The pain was nearly more than he could bear, lancing up through his nerves. It wasn't just his leg now, but was burning like a fire up the length of his right side.

The mound wasn't very tall, about six feet, but it was broad, and the slope of the sculpted earth was mild. It took an eternity to reach his goal, an eternity of moments linked one to the next by bolts of pain, moments in which he knew with a certainty that the droning sound of the choppers would pass overhead, and recede, leaving him there to die, sick and alone. His fears were unfounded. The sound remained constant, if anything growing in strength and intensity.

He reached the uppermost point of the mound and collapsed for a moment–pressing his face roughly into the soil to kill as many of the invading insects as possible, and to try and soothe their bites and stings in the cool dampness. His mind was locked into the urgency of the moment, and before he'd had even long enough to gather his straying thoughts, he forced himself to press away from the mound once more, to lift and roll with his face open to the bright, blistering light of the sun. If they saw him, he wanted to see them as well. He wanted to see the face of his rescuer, or of his death.

It rose above him, at least his height and one half more, bright multi-faceted eyes glistening in the sunlight. Behind it the air was alive with impossibly large, flitting shapes, their long, slick abdomens ending in wicked needles, their antennae fluttering about them curiously. He felt the ground beneath him move more violently, felt the topsoil give way, the brush of slick, hard skin against his own feverish flesh as something slipped free of the mound and launched itself into the air..

He heard chattering voices–voices he knew–familiar words and phrases. The scouts. They were here. Then there was a searing, slamming pain as the stinger slashed through his forehead, pinning him helplessly to the ground and ending his pain. Darkness swallowed him whole.

He voiced a negation, and with strength he'd never called upon before, reserves he should not have possessed, he brought the rifle around and took aim. He didn't see what rose behind him, didn't know the dripping, venomous spike was whistling through the air toward his face. He saw the end of his rifle twitch, felt the recoil as it fired, and saw the glittering jewel-like eyes above him part, shattering and spewing a fountain of multi-colored gore.

The jungle breeze picked up a bit, and the scouts were able to make good time on their return. They had not stayed to witness the final carnage. It was too risky. They needed to get back and to report their success to their leaders, while bemoaning the failure of the mission to the rest of the world.

It would not be difficult to explain how the foreigners had blown the mission with their clumsiness. It was all-too common. None would question them. None would notice the odd, oozing scars on their backs, or the bright intelligence behind their strange, dark staring eyes. None would deny their urging toward another attempt. After all, funds were short, and dead mercenaries were free mercenaries. Another squad could be organized. They would do anything for money, and all they wanted, really, was the war.

Thanatology

Dark Thanatos Looked out upon the Styx
His fingers steepled, looking for some kicks,
His sanctuary bleak and rather dim,
His tenants?–Well–the dead are pretty grim.
He called to brother Hypnos from his throne,
And slapped a rhythm out with ancient bones
A second's light, dark Thanatos did splurge,
As Morpheus' new band cut loose a dirge
A green and glowing blight upon the dead,
Where each could see and know the other's dread
And no man shall ever see,
A lost textbook of Thanatology
Then silence fell and darkness swept away
The stain of light and joy and love–and day
And Thanatos, his hunger sated, said,
There's nothing like a party with the dead...

The Purloined Prose

with Patricia Lee Macomber

The Swan. To most the name conjured images of pristine white feathers, a graceful neck, motion so fluid it mocked the very water in which the bird itself swam. To Edgar, it was an oasis, a hideout, and his temple. He sat at the worn oak and brass altar, folded over a chalice so fogged from age that the light barely penetrated it. His thoughts were turned inward, though his ears were trained on the conversation four stools down. He had no idea he was sitting at the bar with a dead man.

Flickering gaslights dueled with the shadows, chased them across timeworn and tattered walls until they threatened not to exist at all, and then retreated as long dark fingers reached toward the tenuous threads of illumination and threatened to choke the life from them. Edgar's hand trembled, poised over a scrap of paper on which he occasionally scribbled hasty words, some of them his own, some gleaned from the hushed conversation that floated to him from the others. The barman drew near, though he paid no attention to Edgar at all, the scribbler of stolen words, turned on his stool and used his shoulder and arm to shield the paper from the man's sight.

"It has to be a heart, don't you see." The words were slurred and punctuated with spittle but the small, ferret-like man was adamant.

His companion, a large, hulking fellow in a dark coat, his hat slumped in a shapeless mass on the bar at his side, shrugged and downed the rest of his drink in one great gulp. "You are the wordsmith, not I. But I'll tell you this: You'd have a much better time of it if you actually wrote down some of your grand ideas instead of hammering me with them night after night."

"Ah, but I have!" the smaller man said with a wink, patting his jacket. Something crinkled beneath the pressure of his hand. He finished his drink and set the glass down with a clunk. "Every last one. And you'll be laughing out the other side of your face when you see them published, my friend." He slapped the big man on the back and withdrew from the stool, letting his body settle carefully onto his legs and drawing in a large breath to steel him against the effects of gravity.

"Yes, yes! So you keep saying," the big man retorted, eyeing his tottering companion with a mixture of amusement and concern. "Only if you are more adept at writing than you are at walking, though. Now, let's be on our way."

The smaller man nodded. "And while we walk, I shall finish the tale of the heart."

Edgar watched as they made their way to the door, weaving among tables and chairs, dodging other drunken patrons and tilting inward until their shoulders nearly touched. He watched their backs as the door opened, and then slid his eyes around to the barman's pockmarked face. He pressed his hand to the bar for a moment, and then slid it into his pocket, the paper tucked neatly into his fist. He pushed the paper to the bottom and a wrinkled bill was neatly substituted. It was more than the drink had cost; a tidy tip left for the barman's keen inattention.

Edgar's mind whirled in a bourbon fog, but the small man's words had embedded themselves deeply in his mind, and they helped him to focus. Written down–all the stories–written down.

Edgar glanced down the bar and stared at the empty stools the two had vacated, then turned to follow them out of the bar. The words he'd collected rubbed against one another on the crumpled paper in his pocket. Edgar could almost hear their soft scraping, trying to get free and not quite managing it.

The man had talked about the beating of a heart–loudly, like a clock, like a drumbeat pounding behind plaster walls. Edgar never sat too close to the two men, so he never got entire stories–only stolen phrases and words. Now darkness had seeped in that threatened to blot those out as well. If they were already written down, he was too late. If the words had been captured and structured, what was left for him?

The sun was long gone from the sky, and without The Swan's dim light to do battle with them, the shadows closed in tight. It was chilly. Edgar pulled his jacket up and turned the collar so that it wrapped about his neck and broke the wind. He kept his eyes to the ground, watching for potholes in the street, and he walked as quickly as the bourbon would allow. As he walked, his footsteps on the cobbled street found the rhythm of his heart. His pulse grew louder, rushing in his ears, and he stopped, closed his eyes, and tried to gather his thoughts.

He needed to get home. He still had enough oil left in his lamp to write for a few hours, until his bleary eyes could no longer sustain their own weight and the darkness claimed him. His head pounded with the deep resonance of a phantom heart. Edgar turned down an alley that cut off from the shadows of the street into even deeper darkness, and staggered toward his rooms as quickly as his thin, bourbon-clumsy legs could carry him.

Halfway down the alley's length, he caught sight of something lying in his path. It was too far from the walls to be garbage, unless some children had come by and toppled it as a prank. Edgar slowed warily, swinging his gaze to either side as he approached. Then he stopped and stood still as a stone. The pounding that had threatened to blank his mind grew louder still, pressing up into his throat and, thankfully, choking off a scream.

It was a body, and, as he stepped closer, staring in fascination, he saw that it was a familiar body. The small, ferret-like man lay face down in the dirt. His arms were flung out to the side, not as if to catch himself when he fell, but in reaction to something. That something glittered in the dim light, and Edgar saw that it was the blade of a very long, very thin dagger. The hilt stood out from the man's back like a planted cross, and blood ran down the sides of the body to pool on the alley floor.

Then Edgar saw the manuscript, and he forgot the body. The words whispered softly to him, and a stray breeze caught the top corner of one page and threatened to spirit it away. The man's head rested on a pillow of words. Blood had splattered on the paper, and the pool beneath the body seeped upward, encroaching on the white, word-speckled pages.

Edgar took a last glance around and saw no one. He leaned down, lifted the man's head by its greasy hair, and yanked the pages free. He released his grip and watched as the head fell back with a soft, wet thud. A low, wet moan bubbled over the man's thin lips and Edgar drew in a quick gulp of air. It was the last sound Edgar heard as his heartbeat sped and roared. He ran off down the alley, tucking the papers beneath his jacket and fighting to clear the image of that knife, stark and final, pinning the small man's jacket to his spine.

Back in his rooms, Edgar slammed the door behind him and collapsed against its worn wooden surface with a groan. He clutched his coat, and the sheaf of papers, tightly to his chest. The room was sparsely furnished with no more than a bed, a chair, and a small desk upon which rested a stack of clean paper, his ink well and a quill. Edgar made his way across the darkened room, banging his shin smartly on the foot of the bed and crying out softly. He knew better than to make too much noise and risk awakening the other tenants of the building. Grouchy old men flanked him, and down the hall was a woman with hearing so keen she would sometimes complain that the scratching of his quill on the paper was too loud.

He'd filed away her words. He'd filed away the images, as well. He could see her, lying awake, late into the night, her eyes wide open and glaring at the wall that separated them, flinching at each stroke of ink on his paper and dreaming of ways to make him stop.

Edgar flipped the thumb switch on the gas lamp and urged the flame higher, chasing the shadows back into their corners and illuminating the surface of the desk. There was enough fuel for a few hours' work and no more. He couldn't afford to waste a single minute.

He pulled the papers out of his coat and dropped into the chair and smoothed the top sheet out with the palms of his hands. He bent over the page and read, his head cocked to one side and resting on the heel of his hand. The fingers of that hand tugged at his hair as he read, his face trapped between amazement and revulsion.

The tales were wondrous, but the words were lacking. Edgar himself could never have concocted such frightening images from his own limited experience, but the man who'd written these pages had an equal inability to distill those same images into words.

Now, Edgar reflected, the fellow lacked even the ability to sit on his barstool and speak the words for another's benefit. Pity.

Edgar fingered his quill and scowled at the pages. Some of them were spattered with the man's blood, entire words obscured by the thickening goo. Edgar shuddered and tried to read more quickly.

When he had read every word, he sat back in his chair and stared off through the one window in his apartment distractedly. Edgar knew he could do better. He could bring these tales to life. He could bring them to the world.

He glanced at the lamp and saw that the reading had cost him nearly half of his oil. He turned the wick down just a touch, hoping to preserve a few extra minutes of light. He carefully stacked the dead man's pages and glanced around the room. The lack of furnishings also provided a decided lack of good places to hide things. His impatience got the better of him, and he rose, lifted the corner of his mattress, and slipped the manuscript beneath it. He knew he'd have to find a better place eventually, on the off chance they traced his steps from the alley, but for now this would have to do.

He returned to the desk and slid a fresh sheet of paper into the pool of flickering light. He unstoppered his ink, poured a small amount into the well, and tapped the tip of a battered quill against the surface of the desk to clear it.

The dead man's words whirled through his mind. So many images beckoned to him that it was difficult to sort them, or his thoughts, coherently. He decided to go with what was clearest in his mind, and that would be the events of the evening, what he'd heard in the bar. He dismissed the image of the dagger-hilt cross and the small man's back and he began to write.

"The Tale of the Heart."

Edgar stared at the words he'd written, and then frowned. With a quick flourish he dragged the quill through the title and wrote another beside it.

"The Tell-tale Heart." He smiled at the subtle rearrangement and wished, just for a moment, that he could grab the small man from the past, drag him to the desk and show him. It wasn't just the words–it was the way they were used–the art was in their arrangement.

As the flame guttered, threatening to blow out every time he moved, Edgar dipped his quill again, and continued to write.

Morning found him sprawled across the desk, his head resting on the paper and the quill still in his hand. The ink had dried on the tip and the lamp had gone out. As he righted himself, his stiff back crying out in protest, he recalled just when that lamp had betrayed him.

One story done, the next begun. The lamp had given up its last before he'd had a chance to finish. Edgar had plowed ahead, willing his brain to fight through the sleepless fog and finish that second story in the dark. His hand rested on the desk still, awaiting further orders.

No, he could recall no more than a bird, a man and a chair. His brain spun its wheels, trying to wrap itself around that fragmented memory. The lone window admitted a small square of sunlight, which fell upon the paper, taking the place of the lamplight. Edgar smiled a smile that was not his own and chuckled. He cleared the detritus from the pen and began to write. His smile widened with each word.

He wrote through breakfast and lunch, ignored all but one cry for his body to relieve itself of the day's doings. He wrote straight up until two, when he slammed down the quill and gathered together the pages, which now comprised four stories.

He had to eat. He knew he had to rest, and he had other work to do. He stared at the pages grasped tightly in his hands, and frowned.

It wasn't odd for him to drop by the offices of the printer late, and he considered whether, along with the criticism that lay half complete on the desk, buried under the pages, and the blood, he should submit one of the stories. He itched to see them printed, to see the typeset words on better paper than the poor stuff he scribbled on, but.

There was the other man. The stories were changed; there was no doubt of that. The words were Edgar's. Still–there was the matter of the heart. There were the images, the blood-soaked, too-vivid images, not the least of which was the recurring visage of the small man, gesticulating wildly at his friend and spouting his ideas like a madman. What if that friend read the papers? What if that friend, even though he'd never so much as turned in Edgar's direction, knew who he was, and had seen him scribbling the stolen words, night after night? If that man were looking for his friend's killer–or, worse yet, if that man was his friend's killer–what would he do when he read that story?

Edgar's brow broke out in a cold sweat, and he brushed his sleeve across it. He gathered together the sheaf of bloodstained papers and ordered them as neatly as he could, then glanced around the room. There was so little furniture that, under close scrutiny, he saw the close resemblance to a cell. He moved to the bed, lifted the hard mattress, and tucked the papers carefully beneath it once more. Then, with the newly finished stories tucked neatly under his jacket, he headed out of his room and down the stairs.

The sunlight assaulted him, brighter somehow when unhampered by glass. Nevertheless, he lowered his head, squinted shut his eyes, and trudged up the street toward the printers, trying to pry his mind from thoughts of the stories brushing up against him through the linen of his shirt, or the soft moan the man had uttered when his head struck the alley floor.

That night, Edgar dreamed.

He dreamed of New York City. He sat in a chair, facing an older man—an editor. He wasn't sure how he knew this, but he did.

Edgar sat nervously in his chair. He fussed with the pleats of his pants and slicked back his hair, watching the broad-shouldered man in the expensive suit read his stories. They were his stories now and no other's. The only man who could say otherwise was cold and stiff. Besides, while the ideas had not been born in Edgar's imagination, the words certainly had. That made the stories his and thus the fame would be his, as well.

The man read on, eyes widening at one word and narrowing at another. Edgar found it impossible to gauge the man's true response—his vision was oddly vague. Sounds were louder than he could ever remember. As the man read, he put each finished page down on the desk face up, in order. Edgar thought of how this stack would mount up, of how he would have to re-order the pages when the man was done. He wondered which story the man was reading, and why his eyebrows went up and down—why his lips pursed, and then frowned, and then went back to a fine hard slit. Edgar fidgeted with his shoe and frowned.

And then he saw it.

The top page on the stack, the one the editor had just set down, had a small red mark on the upper left corner. It was not a fingerprint, for surely he had seen the man grasp the page by the top right corner. Edgar frowned and looked more closely.

The bottom page in the man's hand sprouted a red spot of its own. It blossomed before Edgar's eyes and grew larger as he read. Edgar swallowed and looked away, blinked three times in quick succession. When he looked back, the red spot was still there and it had grown larger still.

More spots broke out on the pages in the editor's hands. Still more popped up on the stack on the desk. Edgar twitched inside, his stomach tying itself into a huge knot and his eye beginning to spasm. The editor's expression continued to shift through emotions, following the words on the page, but his hands dripped with blood. His fingers smeared the pages, and a steady drip had begun at the edge of the desk, falling from where blood pooled beneath the pages.

Edgar could barely breathe, and that drip became louder. He watched each droplet form, release from the congealed miasma on the desktop, then fall, quivering through the air to PLOP into the puddle beneath the desk.

Then the editor scanned the final page and looked up. He grinned at Edgar. It was the big man. The man who'd been with the smaller one in the bar—and he was smiling. His smile widened impossibly and the teeth it revealed were long, sharp, and hungry.

Edgar screamed.

Edgar sat up with a start. He was shaking and drenched in sweat. It was still dark, and the soft glow from the gaslights shone through the windows, illuminating galaxies of dust motes as they danced in the darkness. Then he heard the *PLOP* and his heart nearly stopped.

Edgar had made tea, and though it would be hours before the city awakened, he could no longer sleep. He had managed to stop the leak in his sink with an old rag, but the echo of that last *PLOP* gave him no peace. He still felt clammy from the sweat-drenched nightmare, and he sat at his desk, pen in hand, brooding.

He was trying to pen a criticism of the latest work by Mr. Charles Dickens, whom he admired, but the words would not come to him. Not those words. The others would not leave him alone, but Edgar had to eat, and he knew he could not sell the stories. Not yet.

"Who is he?" he muttered.

The image of the big man, shaking his head in bafflement at the end of the bar as his friend spewed forth those amazing images in a constant stream, came to Edgar again and again. He tried to remember details. Had the man's hands been calloused? Had he ever come into the tavern with any particular item in his hand that might give a clue to his profession, or his home? Had Edgar ever heard their names?

Bleary eyed, he returned to the work at hand. He had a deadline, and if he missed another, he would no longer have to worry about finding the words at all, because he would be finding a job–and a home–instead. As the sun rose slowly over the city, the scratching of his quill ticked off the moments on the clock, first hesitantly, and then in a steady stream.

———

It was three days later when he finally saw the man, alone at the end of the bar in The Swan. Edgar watched him carefully, trying not to be obvious. He wanted to walk over, offer his hand, and ask where the man's friend was. Get it out in the open. Instead, he watched as the familiar stranger morosely nursed a half-pint and stared at the mirrored wall behind the bar in silence.

It was like being in the theatre and watching a play enacted with one of the main characters missing. The big man's hat sat, just as it always had, on the bar at his side. The stool beside him was pressed tightly against the wood base of the bar, empty with the aspect of having *been* empty for a very, very long time. The barman brought pint after pint, but the two men exchanged no pleasantries, and none of the regulars dropped by to ask questions, or offer condolence.

Edgar drew forth a small sheet of paper from his pocket and placed it on the bar beside his own drink, but when he took his pen in hand, there was no urge to write. The room was filled with subtle sound, low-pitched conversations and clinking glass, the clatter of carriage wheels on the street outside, and the cries of merchants as they closed their shops and carted their wares off the main thoroughfare.

No words. There was nothing for him to borrow, nothing to steal. The empty barstool mocked him. He began to hallucinate forms and movements in the clump of felt the big man called a hat, and each winking crystal goblet signaled to him, and then ignored him when he turned to see.

Then it started. Edgar turned his gaze to the blank sheet of paper, and was horrified to see that it had a spatter of blood near the upper right corner. Had he grabbed this from the wrong sheaf of paper? Had it soaked from his desk somehow, or been shaken free of his clothing after he left the alley?

But no, it was fresh, wasn't it? It was too red to be dried on the paper, and it was spreading. Edgar glanced up to see if the barman had noticed, but he had not. No one had seen–yet. No one knew.

Edgar glanced down the bar at the big man, and as he did so, he felt something on his palm. Alarmed, he glanced down again and gasped, unable to contain the exclamation. The blood had pooled, not soaking into the paper, but leaking out of it. There was a gelatinous globe of deep, red blood quivering atop the paper. It had sprung an inner leak along one side and the trickle that ran out across the bar was what had touched Edgar's hand.

He glanced up again wildly. The barman was walking toward him, and Edgar's heart pounded. He found that he couldn't breathe, and out of the corner of his eye, he saw that the big man at the end of the bar had spun in his seat and had fixed him with a cold stare. When the man slowly rose, Edgar could take no more. He leaped back from his stool, toppling his beer, and spun crazily, nearly veering into a table and two men playing chess on his way out.

<hr />

Shaking his head, the barman swiped his cloth across the counter and mopped up the spilled pint, cursing under his breath and vowing to charge the odd little man who'd spilled it double the next time he came in.

<hr />

Edgar crashed out into the growing twilight and lit off for home. Everywhere he looked things were tinged in red. There was no sound of pursuit, but how far behind could they be?

He reached his rooms and slammed in through the door. The hinges complained, and the knob jiggled wildly about from the sudden fury of his entrance. He shut it just as quickly and ran to the bedside. He grasped the edge of the old mattress and pulled it upward. The pages were still neatly pressed beneath mattress and frame and Edgar let go an audible sigh of relief. Then he grabbed the stack and sorted it roughly. He pulled free those pages from which he had already written and set them aside in a rough stack. As he turned away, the mattress fell back into place with a solid thud.

He crossed to the old fireplace by the door, the room's one ounce of charm. It was sweltering outside, but tonight, the fireplace would add its own heat to the already jungle-like summer night.

Edgar set match to paper and sat back on his haunches, watching as the papers went up in a swift puff of smoke. Cheap paper, it had been, as rough and feeble as any he had seen. And now it curled and charred and wasted away to ashes.

Just before the blackened edges spread inward, Edgar caught site of a small stain on the bottom of one page. Blood. Black devoured red and the stain disappeared as quickly as it had appeared. Then another arose on the blackening surface. And another. Another.

"No," Edgar mumbled into his right fist. "No, no..."

He sank back onto his haunches and rubbed the palms of his hands into his eyes until the pressure nearly made him pass out.

He came slowly back to his senses as evening's shadows lengthened to night. He had not, he realized, bought more oil for his lamp. There was a stationary shop around the corner he knew to keep late hours, and to carry small jars of oil. He might make it there and back if he hurried.

Edgar glanced into the ashes on the hearth, but there was no sign of blood, or dampness of any kind. Only the bone-dust of words. Turning away, he slipped out into the night.

He walked through the moonlight, his head bent low and eyes on his shoes. As luck would have it, the stationary shop was open and the gentleman with the tight mustache and careless hair admitted him long enough to purchase one small bottle of oil. He clutched it tightly to his chest and turned toward home, letting the light of the moon guide him.

By the time he reached his door once more, he felt immensely better. Surely the words would flow and his review would be complete. No more purloined stories or nonsense about bleeding paper.

Once the lamp was refueled and the match struck, the shadows receded and all that remained of the day's madness was a tangy odor of smoke that teased at his nostrils and made him think of fat Christmas sausages. Edgar settled into his chair, took up his quill, and began to read what little he'd written already. Still, his eyes shot to the stack of stories on the back corner of his desk. They were hard to avoid and even harder to remember.

He reached out toward the pages, meaning to glance at the first of them for just a moment, and then paused. He had the distinct and terrifying impression that there was something behind him, something just begging him to turn and see it. He resisted; he tried to force his mind back to the business at hand. The sensation was too strong, and Edgar turned.

A red stain crept out from beneath the mattress. It gathered at the bottom of the sheet, and then traced a thin line to the bottom of the bed frame.

Drip! One drop hit the floor, and then another and the stain worked steadily out from some deep pool of red within, seeping through the aged material until it had spread out to cover the bottom corner of the mattress and formed a large, dark puddle on the floor.

"No! Nonononononononono..." Edgar shut his eyes. He ground his teeth until the sound of it deafened him, and he fought the growing tide of terror for control of his mind.

It's not real, he thought. It's all in your head, man—there is no blood

He turned and faced the desk once more, reaching as calmly as he could manage for the quill. The steady drip of the blood at his back was deafening, and he wondered if the woman who could hear the sound of his quill on paper in the early hours of the morning could not hear this as well. Perhaps she was out now, calling the constable to report the dripping sound

"Not so quick as dripping water, it weren't, sir," she'd say, "but thick-like. Like blood, not so much a drip as a bleeding cut. I heard it through his *walls*."

The dripping was so loud it shook the room, and Edgar dragged himself back from the terror, realizing as he did that the shaking was nothing more than his own nervous tremors. He stared at his hand and thought about the man in the bar and his large friend. He tried to picture them in his mind, only now he couldn't recall if the man had actually been there at all. Perhaps only the larger man had been there. Maybe Edgar had never seen a body in the alley at all, only papers and pages and stories. Maybe none of it had ever happened at all. Maybe there was no pile of stories on his desk, only a stack of empty pages he'd lined up in his own delirium.

He looked back over his shoulder and whimpered. The stain had grown and the puddle beneath was making its way across the floor, spreading into a lake of blood and stretching out to reach for him with glistening red rivulets for talons.

With a cry, Edgar brought the quill down on his free hand. There was a flash of sudden, intense pain, and he felt the kiss of ink and blood as they mixed. With a quick suck of dry air, he glanced sharply over his shoulder at the bed. The blood was gone. He laughed, and the tinny sound echoed off the walls and died slowly.

There never had been any blood. And he had never stolen any stories. The large man at the bar had been alone, and the small man with the face of a ferret and a million stories in his head was a figment of Edgar's own imagination. Like a mantra, he set those thoughts running over and over in his mind.

Yes, that's it, he thought. *It was my own psyche fighting to bring the stories to the surface. My own personal Cyrano.*

153

He looked down and blinked at the droplet of blood oozing from the wound on the back of his hand. The tip of the quill had punctured his skin, and the edges of the cut were growing dark and curling in on themselves. Edgar smiled to himself and began to hum. He couldn't have done that to his hand. It was another product of his imagination.

An even smaller droplet of blood clung to the pen and ran into the ink channel. As he set it to the paper, the blood soaked in and stained it, first a bright red, then pink and finally purple as it flowed away and the ink ruled once more.

Edgar screamed and leaped from his chair, knocking it to the floor and shaking the desk so hard that the lamp nearly toppled in a mass of flames. He righted it with shaking hands before it had a chance to spill the precious oil. Then he stood in the middle of the room, face buried in his hands, shaking harder than he thought possible.

Slowly, he peeked between the fingers of his hands at the words on the page. They were still stained that accusing red. He turned his hand over, and saw that the small oozing droplet was spreading across his wrist. Eyes wide and vacant, he turned to the bed. More than anything in his life he wanted to see clean, white sheets. He wanted to see a slight lump where the mattress rested on the sheaf of stories. Blood dripping from his fingers to stain the floor, he knew that he would not.

The corner of the mattress was a clotted mass of blood. It was blackened at the seam, but the drip was still brilliant red, trickling across the floor and showing no sign of slowing. Soon it would wind its way under the door and out into the street beyond, and someone would see it. He turned back to the desk.

He glanced briefly at the review where it languished, unfinished and insignificant in the shadow of the pages he'd written the night before. Stolen words. The pile of paper was so pregnant with indefinable dread that he expected the corner of it to be soaked with dark ink and bleeding on to the desk.

His hand began to throb, and Edgar walked into his small kitchen and ran cold water over it, washing away the blood and gritting his teeth against the bite of cold water on his suddenly fevered skin.

He wrapped a linen napkin around his hand, covering the wound, and walked to the bed. As he drew near, the room grew hazy, and he stopped. The second he stood still, his sight cleared, and the steady drip resumed. Before he could lose his courage, Edgar leaned in close and gripped the sodden corner of the mattress firmly. As his fingers closed, he closed his eyes as well and gritted his teeth against the sensation.

It never came. The mattress was as dry and hard as it had been the first day he'd laid eyes on it, and Edgar's eyes snapped open as he stared, his heart trip-hammering in his chest. No blood. He lifted the mattress and took the sheaf of papers into his trembling hands.

Feverishly, he thumbed through the pages, removed the top ten and replaced the rest beneath the mattress. He strode to his desk, brushed aside the unfinished review almost absently, and dropped into the chair. There was no sound of dripping blood from behind him. He did not look to see what state the corner of the mattress might be in. He read, and then reread the words, letting them sink into his mind. As he did so, he worried at them, teased them and poked them into a slightly different shape, a more proper tale. It was a tale of obsession, wine, and revenge, and it made his tongue tingle for just a taste of the vine, but he ignored it.

Straightening his desk, his hand still throbbing with pain, Edgar pulled out a new, blank page, and as the lamp flickered and danced, casting its laughing shadows mockingly into the corners of the room, he wrote. He concentrated on the words, and on the paper. The room faded to the background, and it wasn't until two hours later, when he heard an angry banging on his wall, that he looked up from his work.

The hour was very late. The oil he'd managed to purchase was low, and there were only a very few hours until he would be expected to turn in his review. He stared at the paper, pressed to the desk beneath his cramped fingers. There was page after page of writing, neat and ordered, and he barely remembered writing it. He had vague images, and there was something about Amontillado whirling through his thoughts, but...

He straightened the pages and added them to the stack of those he'd already written. Bleary eyed, he reached for his review and for the next hour or so, conscious of every slight scratch of his quill on the page, he worked, glancing nervously at the wall separating him from the old harpy with the bat's ears. He finished with barely enough time for two hours rest, and without even glancing at the corner of the mattress; he fell across it into a fitful, dazed sleep.

The Swan was crowded, and it was difficult to get a good line of sight down the bar. Edgar sat, hunched over a glass of sherry, and glared at the two empty seats across the room. There had been no sign of the large man, and Edgar's hands, wrapped tightly around the stem and body of his glass, trembled. In his pocket he had a single sheet of the small man's manuscript, and on the bar before him, paper and pen. He had written nothing, no captured or stolen phrases.

He was watchful now. At the first sign of the blood, he knew he'd have to write. If he concentrated on the manuscript page in his pocket, went over the story in his head, and wrote the result, everything would be fine. Everything would be dry, free of blood, and they would not stare at him. Their voices would remain muted and distant and impersonal, and they would not accuse him.

An image of the alley surfaced, the man's bloody head leaking onto the pile of paper and he shuddered. He wondered, briefly, if he put the papers back where he'd found them, if the man would rematerialize slowly, blood first, to cover his words, but somehow he knew it was not that simple–and never would be again.

Edgar sipped his Amontillado and thought of the pages, piled and waiting, on his desk. He had more work to do–a criticism and an essay–but first the blood would take its price, and there were many, many pages of the little man's manuscript left to finish. He shuddered again, and downed his drink, signaling the barman for another.

What he feared the most was the bottom of that pile. What would happen when he dropped the last of the manuscript into his fire and watched the blood flow and dry and crackle to dust? When all the stolen words were translated, and the stories piled in a heap on his desk, would they bleed? Would he have to start again, and again, drying it all away through the tip of his quill, or would it be set to rest?

His eyes were slightly sunken, and his pallor had become unhealthy and even paler than was his wont. No one took notice, though they stared at him more closely when he turned in his work at the paper, or when he bought food, oil, or ink. His plan was to write slowly, a little every night, stretching the dead man's words out across the years to come. If he was never without a sheet of paper, and one of the pages of the ferret-man's manuscript, then if and when the blood began, or he was afraid that someone was noticing something, he could translate a few words, or re-read the story at hand.

He was half afraid that if the manuscript brought enough blood, since he'd joined his own to it through the quill, that it would draw him down to his death.

The barman brought his drink, and Edgar cupped it between his palms without looking up. He took a long pull on the sweet, chilled wine and turned to glance down at the empty seats once more. He started, nearly spilling his drink. There was something on the bar, something indistinct and shapeless, but familiar. He shook and drank again, and as he did, he watched. The big man's hat. It lay in its usual shapeless mass on the bar. There was no sign of its owner, but something dark was pooled beneath it.

Edgar shoved his drink away violently, nearly tipping it. He scrabbled for his quill and drew a small bottle of ink from his breast pocket. Opening it and dipping the quill, he began to write with feverish intensity. Outside, the bells on the city clock had begun to ring maddeningly, and though he knew they went on for moments only, the echoing sound lingered. He twisted the sound into something the ferret man had said, something from the page in his pocket.

"The bells, bells bells bells…."

At the end of the bar, where the evening sunlight cast Edgar's shadow down the bar, the lumpy mass that had been a hat dissolved to nothing, and the barman rubbed the smooth, polished surface of the ball unseeing. There was no sound but the loud, insistent scratching of a quill.

Mirrored Hearts

Long barren, sacred temple of my heart
Open now and dripping
Sweet rain.
Cloaked in finery of aching emotion
and flowered vines that
Twine about my soul.
Come to Me, oh priestess of
Mirrored hearts,
Drink the wine that is
My blood,
And let it drain,
Through soul and heart,
and blend with yours…
Lie back on the altar of
bone and fire and
offer yourself,
sacrifice to sacrifice,
The sweet-sharp blade
of my prayer

Slicing soft skin to pierce
Our heart
To drain and savor,
You,
No drop spared as you/I/we run red
Into the temple floor,
As you draw me deep within
The dark cathedral of your eyes
Trade secrets of essence, and power,
and we clasp one another in fluid splendor,
Mirrored hearts,
Feast on one another's dreams
and love as if
Forsaking life.
Come to me oh priestess of mirrored hearts
Drink the wine that is my blood.

Shift

T

he flighty flicker of spooked birds was in her eyes and her
steps were quick and nervous as she picked her way through
the haven. Shapeless lumps half-buried beneath the inadequate
cover of hand-out blankets littered the floor, gathered in a loose
semi-circle around one large metal heater. The dream scratched
at her heart and she shivered. Too cold, always cold, and yet she
had to get away. A longing look at the glowing warmth of the
heater–at her precious space, hard-won, that would not exist
if/when she returned–and she skirted the final sleeping obstacle
between herself and the night.

"Come to me oh priestess,
Of mirrored hearts…"

Her steps quickened as she tried to escape the words lodged
cold and invasive in her mind. The night sky was clear above
her. She bathed in the light of the moon, face upturned, and

behind her the snap of automatic locks offered her to the night with no retreat. The clean, fresh air lightened her heart for an instant and the dream struck again.

"Drink the wine that is my blood."

She shivered and turned toward the park, pulling the shreds of her once fine jacket tightly about her. Her skin prickled with the cold, nipples hardening as they brushed on soiled silk. The dream lapped hungrily at her heart. So long since she'd slept. So long since she'd last been warm.

The moon that moments before had beckoned to her shone brilliantly down to spotlight her as she glided along the empty road, tracing her movements in shadow and baring her, vulnerable, to the dream.

"Lay back on an altar of bone and fire."

She slipped through a line of trees and blended to shadow, blocking the moon's leering eye with their branches. It was only moments before she felt them tremble, calling to her, looming ominous and hungry as they bowed toward the trail–toward her–brushing leaves across her cheeks and grasping with thorns at her hair. She knelt suddenly in the cold trail and let the tears and dreams claim her.

"Offer yourself, sacrifice to sacrifice,"

SHIFT

The temple doors stood ajar and tangled vines dangled like serpents. They clung soft and moist to her skin as she passed. The white linen of her dress glowed blue-white in the moonbeams slipping through the nest of branches dangling

SHIFT

from the withered trees that grew above the massive doors. Her eyes shone clear and bright. Hand clasping the scarab chained to her neck and dangling against her heart, she entered.

Soft voices from unseen sources spoke to her and she glided dream-like through their adulation. She strode smoothly and purposefully down the stone corridor on long graceful legs. Red torch-light glimmered in the depths of her eyes and the voices called to her, now blending–now one.

"The sweet-sharp blade of my prayer
Slices soft skin to pierce our heart."

She felt him deep within and smiled. Thoughts drifted across the screen of her mind's eye, flickering through, away, and she moved forward toward a softer light. It glowed the green of storm and shimmered, as if viewed through a curtain of soft rain. The walls to either side were stained with deeply etched design and time-calloused strength. Faces peered from the crevasses; dreams flickered across mica-coated stone. She felt him again, moving in and around her, and her flesh reacted, pressing against the air that was his breath and straining within her emotionally battered flesh for release within his heart.

"To drain and savor you,
No drop spared as you/I/we
Run red..."

SHIFT

The altar rose, tall, ancient, comforting. His features melted through the stone, melded with the carved visage and back again to her heart. Far above her the scarab embedded in the stone, twin to the one worn over her heart, winked, caught squarely by a shaft of moonlight that invaded the darkness

163

through a crack in the stone roof. In the background, leaking out from the depths of the temple to blend with the night sounds of birds and insects beyond the gates, the voice of running water called to her. She stared at the monument longingly, touched the scarab at her throat again, longingly, tracing lines that matched those above, then closed her eyes, lost in memory and sound and his touch....

SHIFT

The river rolled back and away under the barge, each swell undulating beneath the bound wooden frame and on toward the shore. Crocodiles lounged on each bank, half-concealed in mud, huge glaring eyes locked to the soft bobbing of the barge. They waited, patient as the wind that uncovered the desert floor one grain of sand at a time, uncovering layers and more layers with the patient hunger.

"Fly to me oh Goddess
of Sun and Moon."

She shook her head, rising from the couch that had been brought out on deck for her pleasure, feeling the deck of the barge as it bobbed slowly, graceful steps catching the rhythm of the waves and joining them, stepping lightly and easily.

"Fill the void that is my soul."

She heard his voice calling to her, deep, wide-eyed gaze sweeping the river's banks for his form, the comforting presence of broad shoulders and broader smile. She saw only crocodiles, watching...waiting. She shivered as his words brushed her heart.

"Drain the sacrificial draught…
Of flame and wave."

SHIFT

The waves roared their challenge to her from the rocks far below, shimmering with a soft sheen of moonlight. She slowly tugged the cork free from the wine bottle, arms straining, then the soft pop of release and success. No glass this night. Only the bottle, the cliffs, the waves–his eyes, her heart, dancing over moon-swept water to a distant shore and–back?

She drank, tipping the bottle and letting the rich red wine slide over her lips and tongue, down her throat to bite and grip with glowing talons, warming her and drawing her mind inward. The waves defined her, shivering through the hiss of spray and the pounding of the surf.

"Dark to light ascend,
To dark unfold…"

She rose, wrapping her cloak about her more tightly, the wine forgotten, gazing out over the sea. She closed her eyes, breathing in the cool air, the salt of the wind kissing her tongue lightly and she spread her arms wide, a slender, wingless bird. She stepped from the cliff in a smooth, graceful motion, arms outspread and soaring, out and down.

The wind whipped her hair back and whispered softly as she dove.

"The silk-soft offering of union
Folds tight around one soul,"

She cut through the air in a graceful arc toward the water's surface, sharp reef and surf-rounded stone littering the waves

165

and a deeper, blue-black hole in the center where she would plunge, deep, hugged and cushioned by cold water and the distant, hopeless whisper.

"To hold and comfort you,
No dream spared,
As you/I/we implode.

She sliced the water's surface cleanly, trailing wild, uncontrolled flurries of bubbles in a long ribbon from her lips to the surface. She dove deeper, embraced by water and memory, engulfed in dream, her eyes closed and her mind open.

SHIFT

The walls of the cell were cold and damp, colorless and marbled with mold and fungus. No window marred the smooth surface, which was decorated here and there with steel rings and chains of iron, leather straps, and shadowed corners promised darker gifts.

Her wrists were held tightly by manacles short-chained to the wall above her head, her back tight and naked against smooth stone, legs spread in offering to shadows that reached to carve the letters into soft flesh, sharp talons of memory and sensation, words that said all, and nothing.

"Dream of me,
Oh spirit of pain and love…"

Water dripped endlessly, steady drip-drop-drip of insanity eating into her soul and jumbled among the sounds, lingering in the hollow echo of each drop, his voice.

"Fill the void within my dreams."

Soft skittering in the darker shadows, syncopated back beat to her heart, trip-hammer quick. She shivered. Steady footsteps sounded in the darkness, beyond the stone doorway and she shivered in quick, frantic struggles that accomplish nothing but the tightening of fear's grip on her heart and the punctuation of helplessness.

"Mount the throne
Of ecstasy and angst,"

Leather soles slapped stone in time to the words. She lowered her eyes and waited, dangling tapestry of tender flesh, awash in goosebump textures and cold, colder than she could recall.

"Sink within, disperse,
And pierce my heart."

She felt the words now. No sound, no sensation; they were, and she knew them, nothing more. Her heartbeat slowed and her breathing grew more regular. Her struggles ceased and her bonds became support–her imprisonment protection from…

"The loss of self and solitude
Melts to fluid essence."

Her eyes were closed, but she felt his hot breath sliding over her skin, sensed him near. He did not touch, but fingers brushed the air beyond her flesh, tingled along the lines of her veins and traced the path of her blood.

"Reborn and cast within
a mold of fate …you/I/we

reborn."

The intimacy became too much and she allowed her eyelids to flicker. Light invaded her dark world and his breath departed in a soft whoosh as leather bit air, bit flesh, her scream ripped free and her eyes wide as the lash peeled from her and drew back once more.

SHIFT

The sunlight rose gold-hued and soft over the city skyline and she stepped gently down the overgrown trail. The wrought-iron gates of the cemetery rosè before her, steel-taloned claws raking at the sky and striping the ground with skeletal shadows. She moved between the gates, half-fallen on rusted hinges, careful not to brush the dark metal, colder still than her flesh, her heart.

"Come to me oh Priestess
Of mirrored hearts."

She slipped past row after row of low-cut stones, monuments to the masses, lingering imprints of lives. Each whispered to her softly. Each breathed gentle memories up through the soles of her feet and into her heart, but she heard only one voice clearly.

"Drink the wine
That is my blood."

She stepped through a small, inner gate beyond a lower fence, no less cold, or dark, but more intimate. The gates hung open behind her, and yet there was closeness in the air, boundaries folding about her and the biting edge of finality in the air. She tried to pull the tattered silk, the soiled jacket tighter, but nothing altered the bone-chilling bite of his loss.

"Lay back on an altar,
Of bone and fire."

She stepped to the center of the small clearing, to the long, low-slung tomb of marble, its inscription old now, and worn. She laid her hand on that stone, felt the smoothness, the timeless quality of things remembered, but static. No changes left, only time, and the cold.

She slid onto the stone, laying back, her long hair sweeping across the stone, her shoulder blades pressing against the stone, her heart covering his.

"Offer yourself,
Sacrifice to sacrifice."

She closed her eyes, letting her thoughts drift, falling into the words and the images, remembering. She felt the small scarab, placed about her slender throat by his hand...again and again...time no enemy, but a cycle spent and renewed. The pendant became the single source of warmth in her universe and she slid inward, concentrated herself on that glowing portal as tendrils of thought/mind/soul sifted in and through that gate, calling her to him once more.

SHIFT

She lay on stone, but not the stone of his tomb. The floor of the shelter was colder, surrounded by heaps of rags disguised as human beings, wrapped in the borrowed/stolen tatters of clothing and their battered visions, squatters on a plain of empty dream. Each of them was a world. Each heard his/her own voices.

She opened her eyes and saw one drawing near, stepping carefully between bodies. He made straight for her without hesitation, and she breathed a soft sigh of release. The scarab was so hot it nearly burned her skin.

His eyes met her gaze, cool, calm, cold as ice but filled with the promise of heat.

"The sweet-sharp blade of my prayer,
Slices soft skin to pierce our heart."

He stood directly over her, and she caught the gleam in his hand, felt the soft tug of regret, then peace. The blade rose, worlds fell away. And he, dove-white and shining rose, arms spread and brought together, hot knife sharp and falling, slicing her breast cleanly and diving to her heart. She felt the bite, arched gasping from the stone as the fiery release of herself slicked the floor, his words clear and bright and her hands gripping the wrists, driving the blade deep and true.

"To drain and savor you,
No drop spared as you/I/we
Run red..."

SHIFT

She rose slowly, feeling the warmth and running her fingers gently over bare arms and soft, clean silk. The stone tomb pressed up from the earth, supporting her once more, warm in late-morning sunlight. The air was ripe with the scent of decapitated lily-corpses, slowly wilting remains lining the small grove. She slid to the ground, no longer cold, and turned, tracing patterns on the smooth white stone with her fingers.

His breath caught her, surprise brush on the back of her neck, his large hands resting lightly on her trembling shoulders. His fingers walked slowly around, found the pendant, tracing scarab-beetle legs and he rested his head on her shoulder.

Then he was moving her, turning, bringing her in a slow circle until her gaze found the smaller stone where it jutted from the earth, glinting in the sunlight. Softly gasping she pulled away, kneeling in the soft grass and reading, tracing inevitable words reverently. Two words, numeric patterned symbol of this life she felt–or, did she remember it? Rising, she turned and met his gaze...

SHIFT

Gathered around her now, small worlds pressed tightly one to the next, not colliding, blending instead and circling. Candles flicker in a soft dance and scented smoke from a tiny bowl-fire brazier circles slowly above, whirling captive of ceiling-fan breezes leaving echoed swirls of shadow on the floor as they block the rays of the bare, yellow-bulb eyes suspended above.

Soft voices, murmurs of chanted dreams, bittersweet and longing drift about the room. In the center of the circle she lays on a pillow formed of the faded brocade jacket. Her arms cross her breasts in a cross-hatch hug of finality. There is a hum from the heater, close by, her coveted space now warm and still and those nearby no longer crowding, but watching.

At her throat the candlelight glitters off the scarab, winking at each in the darkness, beyond the veil glimpse at warmth denied. The chant becomes a long soft sigh and trails to nothing. White-coated invaders bully through the circle, voices too loud and eyes too blind to know the ritual in its completion.

Lifted and borne away the shell of what remained and in that motion, soft-gold chain links broken and a tumbling glitter. None moving until the room, once more, is silent, until the space is a vague shadow of her outline…nothing more, and in its center, glowing, lays the scarab, winking like a single, watching eye.

"Come to me, oh goddess
of mirrored hearts."

The voices fall to silence. Small worlds shift and blend and in that shuffle the pendant moves to new hands, eager clever hands that re-bind broken links. Slipping over long, soft blonde hair, lifted to let the scarab rest, pillowed between soft breasts. Her eyes close and she dreams as the voice whispers, calling her home.

Dark Man

The dark man sat, his fingers bent to claws
Ripped the fabric of his soul, and reached
Inside, tearing, rending without pause
Until his armored heart's walls had been breached.
Carefully he sliced out special dreams
And brushed away the mildew and the mold
Then cleaned the space he'd opened, held the seams
Awaiting something glittering, and gold,
Someone who had looked within his mind
And seen those cobwebbed dreams behind his heart
Had worked her way within the ties that bind
To claim those broken dreams as works of art.
She sewed and wove and whispered to his life,
You hold *my* dreams, and you shall call me wife…

For Patricia Lee Macomber

Pretty Boys in Blue and Long Hair Dangling

She tried to compartmentalize it by moving into a single floor of an empty office building. A single long corridor with doors opening to either side. Slide-in plastic labels for each. It might have worked, but the corridor was long, and the offices were too large. The tile on the floor, a checkerboard nightmare turned at diamond angles in the 60s and left to entropy, made her nervous. There were too many windows, and some of them looked back into the hall.

She used curtains to close these off, different colors for each, the insides awash in dangling chains, pendants, photographs, or whatever struck the right muse. Halfway through, she knew it would never work. She'd built her framework on a set number of rooms, and something had changed.

A new muse struck.

Pretty boys in dark blue and long hair dangling–always on the left–wrote obscure Tibetan chants to percussive beats. They met only on the fourteenth day of each month and never in the same place. They drank a particularly pungent Chai variation and recorded their creations straight to digital. Never a CD, never a disk. Nothing but dot-net, and that so clogged with dogma and securely interleavened data that only the initiated could access it. Initiation did not come cheaply, and creating the chants required the full attention of mind and body without karmic dissonance. She wanted to hang with them, but her screen hung on the words 'Transparent to new Bee'. It would take time, and thus, a room.

She would need decorations.

She would have to run cables.

Where to put them? The green room was nearly finished, hung with spider plants that reached floor to ceiling and lost photos of found ancestors, black and whites and color shots from inside brand new wallets. In this office she played only obscure bootleg cuts from unknown bands, removing instantly any sound that might have reached the airwaves on commercial radio. She had books, all hand-sewn, stapled, or pasted together in print runs of one. Works of art, dedicated to creativity. Some of them have been well-reviewed, but only by her, as she owns the solitary copy–no reprints.

Obscurity is its own reward.

Somewhere, she knows, her own book resides on a shelf.

At least, she hopes it does. With one copy only...and no reviews she has been able to locate...so difficult.

The Black Room drips with water in tiny Feng Shui fountains, dyed red and bubbling over rocks, sliding around perpetually spinning balls, dripping down stepped cascades of colored stone. Blacklights, hung in the corners, bring a 'blue-light special' tinge of afterworld to each and every surface. Bauhaus and The Sisters of Mercy glare down baleful and haughty from where they hang beside fan-art vampires–men, women, children with haunted empty eyes and leering, come-hither lips.

The words in the black room reflect blacklight white on dried blood paper.

The leather and dark lace and white enamel required make her ache.

Aching is required to write in the black room.

Each has a connection to the box. The box has 24 port cascaded hubs snaked one to the next in Medsuaesque snarls of cable. There are more strands, and the cascade is endless, but there are no more rooms.

She started in the white room. There everything is organized by sets of rules and lists of infractions. The walls are papered with Strunk & White, pages cut and pasted in grammatical sequence, punctuated by brilliant covers that could have been shorn from their spines and pasted in place but instead are mounted carefully on small clear shelves because each word is sacred. The ties that bind the pages are not made of hemp but strung with gut-wrenched strands of intestinal fortitude. So precise it cuts, the light in this room blinds her and without her shadows she is incomplete.

That room is sealed. Pages written there bear the red pen wounds of frustration, and she knows, (oh yes, she knows), frustration is the key and must be channeled, re-arranged and dug into the page with sharp, swift, surgical slashes of a medium point pen.

And there is a shrine.

Every room has a shrine with names carved or painted, whispered or sent out through digital cables in a quick electronic breath. The creators of literary color and their works. Interviews printed out from the web. Podcasts playing in endless loops. Her words, reams of paper scattered throughout the rainbow, cast at multicolored altars and dusted with the incense of despair. Each bit and piece, chapter and verse written in the proper room, in the proper style, with the proper voice–the accepted voice–the voice that talks to her deep inside gray matter walls when the colors are invoked–the voice that vaguely, somehow reminds her of someone she once new–or was.

Each new color spins the wheel.

Each new inspirational challenge springs potential-to-kinetic in properly formatted leaps of brilliance.

Each rejection spins the wheel, and now?

There are pretty boys in blue with no home because all of the rooms are colored and the halls are bare and diamond checkered all at once. She knows this will be her chance. She will be one of them, the first pretty girl in blue, chanting to the center of cyberspace and fulfilled, but first she needs a room that does not exist.

And so she sits in the center of it all, near the box and the Medusa cables, arms wrapped and twined intricately, crying tears that will run down the wires and into the brain of the box. Tears will clear memory, but an empty, powerless box is of no use to her. She knows it is time to move on and wonders how she will bear to take each room apart.

The colors and the curtains.

The photos and the screens with their podcasts and their sound bytes that nibble her nerves.

The shrines.

She closes her eyes and dreams.

It comes in a vision and her dream-self smiles. Her tingling skin ripples with a soft shiver.

The office building is square, but now she sees a circle. Sliced like a colored pie, each angled segment arranged to fit its rejection perfectly, the box in the center. Plenty of room for pretty boys in blue with their hair dangling (always on the left) and Magenta girls with wolf companions and life stories trickling over sensual lips to dribble ink on vellum parchment–for black and white and Strunk & White–a Carousel of color. Her carousel.

In the center, she will sit and smile and spin the wheel, and all the while, she'll write the multi-colored strands of thought into muse-tight weaves of brilliance.

They will come to her and give her a color and her name will go on the Carousel shrine…

And she will reject them, as all colors must until the paints dry and the hues shift and the brilliance shows its elusive backside to the muse.

Banished

A Three Word Challenge Poem

Banished / Eloquent / Fiend

Grandpa claims his blood runs black,
That the blue veins are just for show,
And the black-light-glowing white hair
Is just for a little while, such a little while,
To an old man once a child,
And Black is the color that once stained
Those locks, ticking clocks, time and locks,
Banished by the white-hot washed-out gleam
Of years shining through skin,
Bone showing through hair,
No one cares, not really, no, but
Not yet time to die, or grow cold.
Death fiend dancing in the air above his head,
Icicle trident poised breast high,
Heartbound and hungry.

David Niall Wilson

Black blood and white hair,
A little while, no one to care.
In the babble of the world,
Only the final silence
Is eloquent.

To Strike a Timeless Chord

The streets were empty vacant and lonely. Clarissa stared out from beneath the old blanket she'd found. She felt the trembling begin to shake its way through her bones once more as the wind wormed its way into her make-shift shelter, pinching at her skin and dragging the warmth from her heart.

She couldn't remember how long she'd slept in alleys, nor could she recall if she'd ever slept in this one before that night. She remembered her mother, and she remembered finding the blanket, days, months, perhaps years before. She remembered a rosy-cheeked little girl who'd given her a pastry to eat. She didn't remember that her name was Clarissa.

She watched nothing in particular; there was nothing that mattered enough, nothing that could have dragged her to her feet, or out of the alley. Not even the hunger that ate away at her insides like a cancer, or the encroaching numbness that slowly claimed her limbs in the name of the steadily dropping temperature could have ever been enough. Clarissa was finished getting up, maybe forever.

There was nothing left–nothing but cold, fear, and the night. She shifted slightly, dragging the blanket a bit more tightly about her legs, and it was then that she heard it.

There was the shuffling of booted feet, the slinking, metallic clang of chains. There was muted, heavy breath that would be hovering, floating on the icy air. She didn't look up, but she knew he was there–knew that he'd seen her, and what it would mean. The air seemed warm, in that second, against the chill of her heart.

As the chain swung through the air, its passing created a hollow, humming note of bittersweet music, biting through the blanket, casting aside flesh and slamming into bone. Clarissa felt herself letting go–releasing the moment. In that second, she heard the note bend, heard it blend to a different sound, a lamenting, weeping note–joined by others to create a chord– and all was still.

Johnny was late getting home after school–really late. He pedaled furiously, forcing his old Schwinn to new limits, new speeds. He knew his mother would understand–he'd been working on the sets for the school play, painting and designing trees and cardboard houses. It was not his mother he was worried about, but his father.

His father did not care about school plays. He cared about very little, in fact, beyond beer, supper, and having his own way, and a part of that was "my family waiting with open arms when I get back from bustin' my ass all day." Johnny had not been there when his father got home, nor would he be there in time for dinner, and that was bad … maybe real bad.

He knew his mom wouldn't let it get out of hand, not while he was in the room, anyway. It wasn't himself he was afraid for.

She always took the pain, always turned his father's anger away from Johnny bore the weight of it herself. Somehow that hurt worse than the whipping would have.

Johnny pedaled like mad–he was racing for his mom, a white knight flashing down the street and through the darkness–a savior.

Bertie Jones was in a hurry too. He'd been at Big Sid's since knockoff, nearly four hours now, and he'd been drinking straight through. He knew how Karen was going to take it, could hear her high-pitched, ear-piercing bitching echoing through his mind already. Sometimes he just had to stop for that beer–those ten beers–just so he could stand to go home.

He slid around the corner, narrowly missing the curb and grinning to himself. He could still handle the old Dodge; that much was sure. Nobody knew these streets like he did–nobody. He slammed off Oak and onto the main drag at Crescent Drive, barreling down the middle lane as he always did and punching the gas. He'd be home in no time. Karen would bitch, but he'd get her to drink a glass of Boone's Farm, loosen her up a bit, and …

Johnny watched the car as it closed in on him. He knew it was in the wrong lane, could see the figure hunched over the wheel clearly, but he didn't move out of its way. His arms wouldn't turn the handlebars. His mind wouldn't respond. It couldn't be happening to him. The man would see, would turn aside and all would be well.

Bertie saw the boy on the bike, and he honked his horn. Damn kids. The punk had plenty of time to get the hell out of the way, though, and if he knew what was good for him, he'd be doing some getting real quick. Damn quick. Bertie punched the gas again and the Dodge shot forward with a screech. Damn, popped it in third!

In slow motion Johnny felt the bike, finally answering the call of his mind, turning to the side. He felt the tires slip, felt his right foot drag behind, felt it skid on the road, bounce up, then collapse. The car never hesitated, never turned aside, and Johnny's last sight, his last earthly vision, was the stupefied, unbelieving stare of the man's eyes, staring right at him, through him even, not really seeing.

The metal of the bike gave quickly under the grinding force of the car, scraping on the road with a high, keening whine that seared its way through Bertie's brain. It was like the screeching notes of super-amplified guitars, the feedback at a mega-watt rock concert, and as he felt the wheel slipping, remembering that he had to steer, that even if the boy was dead, he was not–yet–the whine slipped to a clearer note, a sad note, blending with sounds from somewhere else, somewhere inside, into a chord. Then all was still.

Nigel stared at the pile of white powder on the table. It was there, just waiting for him, waiting for him to get the balls. No fear in that powder, he thought, no hesitation. It knew what it wanted–it wanted him.

He was already flying. There was enough combined Coke and Heroin in his veins to kill three average men, but he knew he'd live. He knew it with bittersweet certainty, knew it as surely as he knew that one day he would die.

Why not today? Why wait? He'd seen the edge, how about the other side? A little Morrison philosophy for the masses, a tribute, if you will, to those who'd gone before. Truly gone.

He scanned the walls of his apartment, letting his gaze linger on each photograph, each album cover, each memory and each pain. Melissa. She was gone, too, more truly gone than even Morrison, because Nigel could follow where ol' Jim-bo had gone, Melissa wasn't coming back.

There had been one time, with enough Coke, when he'd thought that one of the endless string of groupies that had paraded through his room and across his bed was Melissa. His warped-out mind had told him that she'd slipped in with the other tramps to win him back.

Then reality had kicked him in the balls, slamming back into place with finality and mocking laughter. The drugs had faded, the girl had been so stoned she had to be carried to a taxi and sent on her way, and the memories that had surfaced in her passing still lingered to tap and chisel away at his sanity. Time to go now, before that eroded, too, and he got locked away where there were no choices, no doors to the edge or windows to the abyss.

Nigel Waters, man with everything, man with nothing. Already gone. All that remained was the image, the plastic mannequin image he'd formulated to hide himself from the cameras and the world. Now it was empty, and they didn't care. Image was everything–who'd said that? Some athlete, he thought vaguely, someone who didn't understand the truth of it.

The heroin glittered in the dim light, mocking him, calling out to him. He felt his hands moving as if in a dream, following the commands of his mind, but not at the time they were issued. He was fascinated–possessed. He managed, somehow, to get the hypodermic to rest in his hand without dropping it, and he brought it to the arm of the chair.

Setting the needle aside, he reached for the red bandanna that lay across his knee. A dirty red bandanna. He smiled crookedly. Still holding onto that trademark, that rock, roll, and who-gives-a-damn image. Shit, he should have looked through the drawers to see if one of Melissa's silk stockings were still around. That would've looked better in the magazines.

He wrapped the bandanna around his bicep, pulling one side tight with a trembling hand, the other with his teeth. Not a rubber hose, but it would have to do. He'd been searching veins out of skin for years–no problem. He'd find one. He always had.

He grabbed the spoon next. It had some residue left from his previous hit, but he splashed it onto the floor, momentarily fascinated as light glittered across the arcing droplets. Shaking his head, he lurched to the table once more, nearly knocking the entire mess to the floor, and grabbed the bottle of Jack Daniels that sat there. He'd always wanted to try this. One shot left, so to speak, might as well be the Jackmeister.

He tipped the bottle back, taking a big slug and letting it wind its fiery path down his throat to his stomach. Then he tipped it once more–slowly, catching a spoonful of it and tossing the rest of the bottle aside where it shattered against the wall and dripped down to form an alcohol-abusive stain on the carpet. Didn't matter, not his problem anymore.

The amber liquid in the spoon quivered once, twice, and then was still as he rested it beside the needle on the chair's arm. And now for the flames and the finale, the grand show-down.

He grabbed the spoon again and began to heat it with the candle that burned beside him, mesmerized by the flame, watching the red-gold flickers rise and fall, shifting about with a life of their own. It wasn't until the handle of the spoon began to get warm that he remembered what he was doing. Shit.

He reached into the pile of powder and grabbed a large pinch–a very large pinch, dropping it into the whiskey. He watched it beginning to dissolve, then said, "What the hell," and tossed in a second pinch. He worked it all around with the tip of the needle, stirring and crushing, creating.

He was creating a way out, a doorway to another place. When it was all one consistency he dipped the needle in and drew up several CC's of the mix–several too many. The bandanna, almost forgotten by then, had done its work, cutting off the flow of blood to his hand.

"Good thing I only need one for this," he said with another grin. He stared at the largest poster on the wall. Jim Morrison stared back at him, one hand out in front and beckoning, calling out for him. He plunged the needle through his skin.

"I'm coming, damn you," he said. As the drugs hit him, he slumped to one side, his eyes spinning back into his head, which lolled backward aimlessly.

The spoon and the needle crashed and tinkled to the floor together, a brittle sound that rang through his fading senses like the peal of a broken bell, the notes of a twisted banjo. It all blended then, a single note, a single tone, blending with others that rose from his drowning mind to form a chord. Then all was silent.

―――――――

The hospital bustled with activity. There were quiet wards, of course, but it was never quiet in this one. There was too much happening, too many smiles and cries, surprises and miracles. Sandy pushed her cart quickly down the hall and stopped before room 112.

She peeked around the corner first, making sure she was interrupting nothing. She'd been to the La maze classes, knew what they taught people in there. There was no telling what the couple inside might be up to, nipple massage, something more intimate. Anything that would help to hurry the magic moment, anything that would bring an end to the waiting.

The woman was sitting up, the blanket held in white knuckled fists, and the husband looked up quickly as she came in, a nervous smile on his face.

"I think it's time," he said breathlessly, turning back to gaze into his lover's eyes. "I think he's coming."

Nodding, Sandy moved quickly, buzzing the desk and at the same time moving to the foot of the bed. With practiced hands she lifted away the blanket, eliciting a small gasp from the mother to be, and leaned forward to check.

No doubt. This one was coming, and coming fast. There would be no hesitation, no waiting for the world to come to him, he was ready to come to the world!

A nurse hurried in, the doctor not far behind, and Sandy moved aside with a smile, taking the woman's free hand in her own and murmuring encouraging words. The fingers she held tensed, but the young mother's eyes were clear and bright.

It took only moments, and as the father moved to the side, staring lovingly down into the pinched little face, the sound came, beautiful as any church choir, bright and full of light and life. The first sound, the "cry of life," as Sandy liked to call it.

The baby's cries blended with the happy sobs of the mother, the mumbling, incoherent babbling of the father, the compliments from nurse and doctor alike, forming a note of hope, a harmony–insinuating themselves among other sounds that seemed to float in the air to form a chord …

The old man sat on the street corner, as he always sat his flute in his hand and his battered hat turned up on the ground before him. The dark lenses of his glasses reflected the lights of the early evening, the glowing neon, and the passing headlights. If he could sense their presence, he made no sign.

He held his instrument like a lover, caressing the length of it, his fingers flickering and dancing across the keys. His music was sad, but moving. You could see his world through that music, if you listened long enough, could imagine others. It carried pain, love, the past and any number of futures, all cascading among its soaring notes.

Lovers stopped to listen, staring at the stars and forgetting the concerns of the day. A prostitute leaned against the lamp post on the corner, watching and dreaming, stealing back a moment of time no longer her own.

Cars came and went, snatching silvery bursts of sound through open windows and carrying them off to other places. Echoes of the sound drifted through the alleys, across the streets and into windows. Then it was silent.

The old man cocked his ear to one side, listening intently. None could hear what he heard, but then, none could see what he saw, either. He lived inside the music, in places far and near, but hidden. He frowned, and then grew sad. His eyes drooped and moments later he shook his head, as if in pain, or disgust.

He lifted the flute once more, and a smile crept back across his face. Listening for just an instant more, he chose his moment and added his own note, a single crystal-clear tone, to those he heard.

Those nearby were amazed. They saw a blind man, and a flute, but they heard so much more. A chord, a single chord–sad with ending, bitter with defeat, alive with promise. It was no sound born of an instrument, though none could say from whence it came. It rang through the night, catching at hearts and turning heads, and then faded away to another melody entirely. Soon all was silent.

The old man let the flute drop to his lap, and he sat in that silence, dreaming his dreams and letting the music play on within his soul. Darkness claimed the city, but at its heart a light burned bright and steady.

End Of Days

A Three Word Challenge poem

Antidisestablishmentarianism / Pluto / Orange

In Ireland, where William of Orange laid his hat,
Beyond the reach of Pontiff's Rome,
The Church of England came, and spoke of God.
And though the people cried, and railed, and fought
Against this new encroachment on their home,
The King, in England, only found them odd,
And tried to force them to his iron rule.
And that is why, in Irish Schools,
While disappointing Clyde Tombaugh,
By denying the 'planet' Pluto,
When spelling, teachers must insist...
Antidisestablishmentarianism does not exist

And thus do we approach,
The end of days.

Etched Deep

Ethan sat back in his rocker and propped one booted foot on the porch rail. He watched the sunset dribble down behind the trees. Trails of color streaked the clouds. The steady creak of the rocker emphasized the silence. Now and then he heard one of the animals shuffle in the barn.

The shotgun lay across his knees, barrel angled out over the yard toward the tree line and the butt nestled close in to his waist. He reached down to the cooler at his side, lifted the rusty metal lid, and fished out a bottle of beer. It was cold. Ice water dripped onto his hand and his pants as he lifted it and twisted off the cap.

A loud, muffled thump sounded inside the house. Ethan paused, cocked his head to the side, and listened, but the sound wasn't repeated. He took a pull off his beer. A few feet to his right Jake sprawled in a mass of wrinkles and fur. The dog watched Ethan sleepily. Ethan leaned back, closed his eyes and let the cool evening breeze brush him back through the years.

He couldn't remember a time when he hadn't owned a dog. His father gave him a puppy for his second birthday. Casey, they'd called her. Ethan's sharpest memories of that dog began with the warm, comfortable scent of her fur and the deep, trusting gleam in her eyes.

There were other memories as well. He remembered the scent of the forest in the early morning, when the dew still dusted the grass and the shrubbery that lined the trails. He remembered the sour smell of oiled gun metal, and the acrid tang of powder. He remembered Casey, baying and thrashing through the trees, his father's heavy footsteps and slow, careful voice.

Ethan's father lived and died in a cut and dried, black and white world of absolutes. There were no gray areas. There were no shades or demilitarized zones. A thing was what it was, a man did what he had to, and a boy listened to his father.

Casey grew faster than Ethan, and by the time he was six, she had given them three litters of fine dogs. Each grew to either hunt at their mother's side, or to be sold in the town and hunt with another man's family. It was what they were born to, and she dropped them like clockwork. She carried the small, furry bodies into the crates Ethan's father prepared for her, lined with hay and scraps of cloth. She bathed them until they were glossy and when they were hungry she rolled onto her side and offered herself without question. When there were no puppies, she slept with Ethan, and his father allowed it.

When Ethan was eight, Casey was getting a little long in the tooth. She hadn't had a litter of puppies in over a year, but then she got pregnant. Ethan worried over her, fussed with the crates himself, and waited. The dog grew nervous and restless, but they chalked it up to the coming litter. The days came, and went, and then the final litter was born.

Another loud thump drew Ethan from his daydream. He glanced at the house. No one appeared in the doorway. He heard muffled voices, but they died away. There was a third thump, and someone cried out sharply. He thought he heard a low wail after that, but the breeze kicked up and the sound was lost. He set the empty beer bottle on the porch floor carefully and extracted a second icy, dripping bottle.

Casey carried that last litter, only three pups, into the crate, just like she'd done all the times before. She washed their tiny heads until their fur shone bright and she nuzzled them close to her when they whined. She fed them and watched over them, and they grew, even the sickly, smaller one that Ethan had resigned himself to losing. They grew, and as they did their hunger followed suit. Their teeth sprouted white and sharp, and they grew insistent when it came time to eat.

Ethan had seen Casey wean her whelps again and again, nipping them and driving them away, rising to run off in a shiver of loose skin and swollen teats, nudging them toward the bowls of milk-soaked food his father provided. She had always been patient and careful. This time she snapped. One of the pups lingered too long when she growled at it, and her jaws closed over its tiny head in an instant. One flashing moment of blood and sound, and it was over.

Ethan remembered that moment with a clarity he'd seldom experienced. He still saw Casey, whining, nudging the dead puppy with the tip of her nose as if in apology, wanting it to stand and come to her, to feed and grow strong. Her eyes had been so full of misery and emotion–so human–that Ethan wanted to scream every time the memory surfaced.

His father took the other two puppies away after that. They were ready to eat solid food, and he kept them clear of Casey until they were old enough to take care of themselves. She never went after them again, but something inside her had snapped.

Two weeks later, Ethan's younger sister, Jenny, walked too close to Casey's tail. The dog turned like brown lightning. Her eyes were crazed with mad anger, and she snapped. She only caught the material of Jenny's skirt; the girl was also quick, but it was enough. Ethan's father beat Casey near to death that day, and everything in Ethan's life shifted. Sometimes you grow up slowly and learn over years of trial and error. Sometimes it's a snapshot in time, one moment a boy was young and the next as old as the hills.

A wail rose from the house and Ethan half turned in his seat. He saw Benjamin, his eldest, press his nose to the inside of the screen door, but the boy didn't come out. He watched his father through that screen, followed the arc of the beer bottle as it was tipped back again, and then the boy disappeared. The sound of someone crying softly joined the eerie voice of the breeze.

Ethan drifted back one last time. Ethan always hunted with his father. They gathered the dogs, strode slowly off into the woods that lined their pasture, and walked together in silence. They hunted for food, and they shared the hunt for companionship. It was the strongest bond the two forged over many years, but the night after Casey snapped at Jenny, Ethan's father went alone.

His father had spent extra care on his shotgun that night. The barrel was cleaned and oiled, the stock polished. Each load was pulled from the case and examined before disappearing into the many pockets of the old hunting vest Ethan knew so well. He knew the scent of that vest from sitting on his father's lap. He knew the places it had been torn and mended. He knew where things had been spilled on it, and the exact point on the collar where a drop of blood from his own first kill had soaked in and stained the material a dark brown.

Ethan had carried his own gun to the porch that evening, but his father had just shaken his head.

"Not tonight, son," he'd said.

No explanations were ever offered, or expected. As the sun set, his father headed off toward the woods. Ethan sat on the porch, watching. Casey trotted along at his father's heels, and this was odd. She was old, and she rarely accompanied them. When she did, it was always with some of the others–faster, younger dogs that could run an animal down, or tree it. Casey had grown slower, and generally kept close to home. Ethan watched until both man and dog were out of sight.

He remembered the sunset glinting off the oiled barrel of his father's gun. He remembered the way that same light shimmered off Casey's fur. Hours later, when all hint of the sun had left the sky and the night breezes set tree branches dancing in the shadows, his father returned. Alone.

Ethan remembered that lined face, the vacant stare that presented itself in the pale light of that long-ago moon. His father walked up and sat on the porch. He didn't say anything at first. Ethan wanted to scan the trees. He wanted to ask about the dog, but something hung in the air that clotted in his throat. He kept his silence, and eventually, his father spoke.

"Sometimes things change. There are things inside that guide us, and no matter how hard we work to keep them whole and safe–sometimes they break. They snap like dry twigs and even if you're very quiet about it, people will hear that sound. Things you try to avoid come back to stare at you and to see what happened.

"Casey was old, son." His father spun to him then, and held his gaze. "She was a good dog, but that last batch of puppies was too much. She was broken inside, and there's nothing you can do to mend such a break. She killed that puppy–that was the start. She would have killed your sister if she hadn't missed–or you–or taken a chunk out of my leg. She couldn't help it–the thing that kept her steady was gone. The broken thing inside poked and prodded at her until she snapped, and it would have done it again."

Ethan remembered the burn of tears in his eyes. He remembered the cold clutch of invisible fingers around his heart, and the way his breath caught in his chest and couldn't get free. He said nothing. His father turned away, and fell silent, staring out over the distant trees. His gun rested beside him, barrel leaned on the porch rail. Ethan remembered it as a giant finger, pointing somewhere he'd never go again. He thought of Casey's warm fur, and her huge, soulful eyes. He'd seen the lines in his father's face differently for the first time, recognized them for what they were. Pain had etched those lines, deep pain held inside for too long. It was a lesson, the sort left unspoken, yet never forgotten.

The screen door creaked, and Ethan drained his beer, half-turning toward the sound. Rebecca pushed the door open just far enough to slip out, and let it close behind her. She stood, staring at the interlocking boards of the porch floor. After a moment of silence, she spoke.

"Jimmy's arm is hurt. He…"

Ethan held up a hand, and she fell silent. He lifted the lid of the cooler, drew out two more bottles, opened the first, and offered it to her. She stepped forward slowly, as if dazed, and took the bottle from his hand. He opened the second bottle and took a long pull. He still heard the quiet sobbing from inside, and he felt the press of Benjamin's face to the screen, though he didn't turn to look.

"Beautiful night," he said.

Rebecca turned and stared at the blood red drip of the sun as it melted beyond the trees. She nodded and sipped her beer. It was warm, but she trembled. Ethan reached out and touched her arm, remembering other nights–other times. She was still beautiful. He watched the dying daylight play over the dulled highlights of her hair. She still had the old defiance in her stance, the spark that had won his heart, but now it was cockeyed. She stood just a little off balance, as though waiting for some unseen thing she kept in the periphery of her sight to strike.

They drank in silence. When the bottles were empty, Ethan rose. He turned to her, gave her a quick hug, and leaned in close.

"Walk with me?" he said. Not really a question.

Benjamin stepped onto the porch. He held the screen half open.

"Papa?" he said softly.

Ethan stopped and turned.

"You want me to come?"

Ethan shook his head. "Not tonight, son," he said.

Benjamin stood on the porch and watched them go. He saw the sunset glinting off the oiled barrel of his father's gun. He remembered the way that same light sometimes shimmered off his mother's hair. He watched until they were out of sight, then watched a bit longer, then turned back to soothe his brother's tears.

She nodded again, setting her still half-full beer bottle on the porch rail. Ethan slid his arm around her shoulders, and they stepped off the porch together. He kept the barrel of the shotgun angled down and away, the weight comfortable in his hand.

Longhaired Puppies

He went because he heard them cry,
Like puppies in a darkened empty room,
He went because he couldn't let them die,
Alone, beneath a waning weakened moon
The stairs stretched down to shadows, and he bent
His head to keep from brushing blackened walls
The candle in his hand lit his descent,
But danced and guttered in the stagnant air
Their voices died before his steps grew near,
His heart slowed, and he whispered in the dark
But bones and dust once flesh, they cannot hear
And longhaired puppies in white skirts don't bark
He sat among their ghosts and softly cried
His puppies broken bones close by his side...

Unique

His shaved head and bright blue eyes stood out in the crowd. She saw him coming, repressed the urge to angle her steps away, or to bolt, and watched. His arm was bandaged, wrapped tight in gauze and once-white tape. A dark patch in the center had grown brown and she knew if he pulled that bandage loose, skin and dried blood would accompany it.

She drew her gaze up, but did not meet his. Instead she concentrated on something dangling from a chain about his neck. It was oddly shaped, like a leaf, and it had little weight. As he walked, it lifted into the air and seemed to flutter back to his chest, only to lift again.

He was close. She knew she'd have to bolt or meet those eyes. He stopped directly in front of her and dared her gaze to lift. Instead, bolder than she felt, she leaned in close to inspect the pendant.

It was thin, like parchment. On the surface in dark ink was a dragon. Through the center of the design there was a sword. Above the dragon, in a semi-circle, she saw words.

"Death before dishonor"

She glanced up into his snake eyes and was caught. She stood, unable to run, trying to make her lips form an explanation, or a question, but barely able to breathe.

"I got a tattoo once," he said. "I was unique. It was a statement of my individuality."

She breathed a little deeper. His voice wasn't threatening, or loud. He almost whispered.

"Can I see it?"

He continued as if she hadn't spoken. His eyes pierced her and squirmed around inside her head as she heard, and tried not to hear, his words.

"Everyone thought the tattoo was cool. Then another guy got one, and another. I walked in an ocean of tattoos, and I was lost."

She repeated her question, still a whisper.

"Can I see it?"

"You already have. I'm told some men wear their heart on their shoulder. I wear my individuality on a chain."

Her hand came to her lips unbidden. If her legs hadn't been made of rubber and cemented to the Earth, she would have backed away, and away, and turned and run, but she didn't. Instead, she reached out and brushed her fingertip over the dragon. For the first time, she smelled the bandage, ripe and pungent. She gripped the dragon gently and met his gaze.

"You are the only one?"

He nods.

"It only hurts," he says, "when I dream."

About the Author

David Niall Wilson is a USA Today bestselling, multiple Bram Stoker Award-winning author of more than forty novels and collections. He is a former president of the Horror Writers Association and CEO and founder of Crossroad Press Publishing. His novels include *This is My Blood, Deep Blue, Sins of the Flash,* and Many More. His most recent published works are the collection *The Devil's in the Flaws & Other Dark Truths,* the novella *When You Leave I Disappear, and t*he short novel *Closing Time at the Sunny Side Up,* available now from Shotgun Honey Press. David lives in way-out-yonder NC with his wife Patricia, 12 cats, and a chinchilla named Pook-Daddy.

Bibliography

HWA Bram Stoker Awards

2008: "The Gentle Brush of Wings" (*Defining Moments*) — short fiction — **winner**
2008: *Defining Moments* (Sarob Press) collection — **nomination**
2008: *Storytellers Unplugged* (by Joe Nassise & DNW) (Storytellers Unplugged) nonfiction — **nomination**
2004: *Roll Them Bones* (Cemetery Dance) — long fiction — **nomination**
2003: The Gossamer Eye (by Mark McLaughlin, Rain Graves & DNW) (Meisha Merlin) poetry collection — **winner**

Novels

This Is My Blood (1995)
Except You Go Through Shadow (1997)

The Temptation of Blood (2004)
Deep Blue (2004)
The Mote in Andrea's Eye (2006)
Ancient Eyes (2007)
Hallowed Ground (2011) with Steven Savile
Nevermore: A Novel of Love, Loss, & Edgar Allan Poe (2012)
Darkness Falling (2016)
On the Third Day (2016)
Remember Bowling Green: The Adventures of Frederick Douglass: Time Traveler (2017) with Patricia Lee Macomber
Gideon's Curse (2017)
Maelstrom (2019)
Jurassic Ark (2021)
Closing Time at the Sunny-Side-Up (2025)

The DeChance Chronicles

Heart of a Dragon (2013)
Vintage Soul (2009)
My Soul to Keep & Others - The Origin of Donovan DeChance (2011) [SF]
Kali's Tale (2012)
A Midnight Dreary (2018)

Tales of Old Mill, NC Featuring Cletus J. Diggs

The Not Quite Right Reverend Cletus J. Diggs & the Currently Accepted Habits of Nature (2011) [SF]
The Not Quite Right Reverend Cletus J. Diggs and the Crazy Case of Foreman James (2013)

O.C.L.T.

The Parting (2012)
The Temple of Camazotz (2011) [SF]
Crockatiel (2015) [Cletus J. Diggs crossover]

The Scattered Earth

The Second Veil (2011)

Star Trek: Universe

Voyager #12 - *Chrysalis* (1997) also appeared as:
Translation: *Puppen* [German] (1998)

Stargate Metaverse

Stargate Atlantis #15 *Brimstone* (2010) with Patricia Lee
Macomber

White Wolf World of Darkness

Dark Ages: Vampire

Dark Ages Clan Novel: *Lasombra* (2003)

<u>The Grails Covenant Trilogy</u>
To Sift Through Bitter Ashes (1997)
To Speak in Lifeless Tongues (1997)
To Dream of Dreamers Lost (1998)

Wraith

Except You Go Through Shadow (1997)

Exalted

Relic of the Dawn (2004)

Novellas

Roll Them Bones (2003)
The Preacher's Marsh (2008)
The Dun WHAT? Horror (2021) [Cletus J. Diggs DeChance
Chronicles crossover]
When You Leave I Disappear (2024)

Collections

The Fall of the House of Escher & Other Illusions (1996)
Defining Moments (2007)
Ennui and Other States of Madness (2008)
The Devil's in the Flaws & Other Dark Truths (2023)

Curious about other Crossroad Press books? Stop by our
website: http://crossroadpress.com
We offer quality writing
in digital, audio, and print formats.

Subscribe to our newsletter on the website homepage and
receive a free eBook.